FAULTY FALLON

A. MONIQUE

Carla,
Thank you
for your support!

A. Monique

❀ Created with Vellum

ABOUT THE AUTHOR

A. Monique was born and raised in East Chicago, IN. She still currently resides in Indiana with her family.

A. Monique discovered her love for books and good stories in all different genres at the age of thirteen, with a special interest in Urban Fiction; even writing some of her own short stories and poems. It wasn't until after beta reading and the encouragement of friends and family, that she discovered her own talent.

FAULT·Y

/ˈfôltē/

adjective

working badly or unreliably because of imperfections. (of reasoning and other mental processes) mistaken or misleading because of flaws. having or displaying weaknesses.

CHAPTER 1

The old saying goes, "When life throws you lemons, you should make lemonade." Well, I say, fuck life and its lemons. I laugh to myself as I think, *at this point, I'm ready to throw those bitches back!*

My name is Fallon Jax. I've been through more than my fair share of bullshit. If I had to take a guess, I would say it started with the man who was supposed to be considered my first love. Yep, my womanizing ass Daddy. "Papi" is what the streets called him. I simply referred to him as Fonzo.

Fonzo Fernando Jax was his government name, and yes, he was just as attractive as the name sounds. My grandmother, Lord rest her soul, gave him that name.

Fonzo was 6'5" with a body that could make any woman lust over him. He also had the prettiest teeth you could imagine on a man. He usually wore his thick mane in two French braids, straight to the back.

His mother, Xiomara, must've had an intuition that the half-Black, half-Cuban offspring she bore would give the ladies hell. My mother was included in that number.

Don't get me wrong, my father never did anything out of the way towards me. He just simply chose the street life over his daughter. His only daughter, if I might add. Fonzo had a total of six children with six different baby mamas. He had five boys, and then me, the only girl.

You would think that I would be my daddy's world, however, he never really gave two fucks about having a daughter. He wanted to be on some "King" type shit, so having five sons gave him the army he needed to take over the streets.

One good thing I could say about Fonzo was that even with him being absent emotionally and physically, he never lacked financially. My mother, Stormy, wouldn't have had it any other way.

I have pretty decent relationships with my brothers, but if we're being honest, they were all either focused on the streets or their bitches. I had six men in my life and still felt vulnerable and open to the influence of fuck niggas.

The ones who knew I was off limits always wanted to try their hand with me. I snuck around with a few, but when Fonzo or one of my brothers found out, they would beat the niggas' ass. Or even worse, making some disappear.

That didn't stop shit, though. I was on a search for something. I didn't know what at the time, but I would soon figure it out.

As cliché as it may sound, Fonzo and my brothers were arms distributors. In layman's terms, they sold guns. They supplied everybody in the Midwest with the guns and heavy artillery they needed. The streets loved them, mainly because they had every gun you could imagine, including military grade weapons.

Everything was going good until some weak ass niggas started snitching.

One by one, Fonzo and "The Boys" started catching cases. And one by one, they were getting locked up and sentenced to some lengthy bids. They had the best lawyers money could buy, and they all assured them that they would do a little time to satisfy the government's itch to lock them up and anybody else up for the many crimes committed in the Midwest. The lawyers guaranteed that they would all be free in no time.

. . .

I HAD a suspicion that my mom was Fonzo's favorite baby mama — mainly because she was fine, and I don't mean basic fine. She was FINE FINE.

My Granny Mozelle, whom over the years I'd lovingly referred to as "My Girl," had the right idea, giving my mother a name like Stormy.

Standing at five feet and four and a half inches, and she will curse you out about not adding that half, my mother was black mixed with Jamaican. She had the smoothest chocolate skin you'd ever laid eyes on, a round face, jet black hair, and beautiful smoke gray eyes. No one knows where they came from because no one in the family had them but Stormy and me.

I favored both my mother and Fonzo to some people. I ended up with my mother's milk chocolate complexion, and Fonzo's long, thick, jet-black mane. I believe that I am the spitting image of my mother, eyes included. One thing about the women on my mother's side of the family was that none of us were a size two. Stormy was a gorgeous size eighteen, and I could easily jump my ass into a fifteen or sixteen.

Fonzo and my mother met when she was green and seventeen. She thought she had found "the one" — that was until she found out that Fonzo treated every girl like she was special. She learned quickly, just not quickly enough, because by the time she figured it out, she had already become pregnant with me.

My mom loved Fonzo with all of her heart, shit, she probably still does till this day, but she won't be nobody's fool.

She took great care of me; she never missed a moment with me growing up. That's another reason I think she was Fonzo's favorite baby mama. She was and is, always on her shit. She always had a job and never settled for just any behavior from him. Her respect was demanded. For that, he always made sure that we were beyond straight financially.

Sometimes I sat back and wondered how I was the opposite of my mother — how I still managed to fall for the okey doke with these hood niggas. The fucking irony!

CHAPTER 2

I wasn't big on running the streets as a teenager; outside just wasn't my thing. I had plenty of friends who loved the streets, though.

At sixteen years old, I had friends whose mother's didn't give two fucks about what they did and where they went. My best friend Tia's mom was like Stormy, and she didn't play.

So, when my other friends met boys, they always felt the need to "hook me up." I wasn't necessarily looking for a boyfriend, but if one came my way, so be it.

That brings me to my first mistake. His name was Dominik, and this fucker had the nerve to share the same Zodiac sign as me — Taurus. That should've been the first red flag.

My friend, Karess, gave Dominik my number. I should've known from the beginning that he would be trash because Tia got a bad vibe from him. She'd never steered me wrong.

Things started off smoothly with me and Dominik. We would talk on the phone all night and go out on dates on the weekends. He was a little older than me, two years to be exact, so he was on his way to graduating high school, while I had two more years to go.

One of those date nights turned into me losing my virginity. I still don't know why I chose THAT nigga, but hey, at the time, I thought he was my forever boo.

Immediately afterwards, I felt like I had made the wrong decision. Something just didn't seem right.

Once I popped my little young cat on Dom, he turned into a crazy nigga. He started popping up at my school, a calling me a hoe whenever I didn't pick up the phone fast enough, and even making me feel bad for not wanting to be around him every single day.

The last straw was him popping up late as hell at my house because I didn't answer the phone. I guess the nigga had a death wish because Stormy was home.

"Why, Lord?" was all I could say when I heard my mama curse that boy to filth.

Of all the people in the world, he chose to wake Stormy Swilley out of her beauty sleep at eleven o'clock at night — on a school night, nonetheless!

I quickly jumped up and ran to the door. "Mama, what's going on?"

She responded with, "Fal, who the fuck is this nigga at my door this late? And why are you fucking with grown niggas who clearly have no respect for your household?!"

Imagine my surprise when Dominik looked me square in the face and said, "You better had been here," and walked off.

If my mother hadn't been standing there, he would've seen a very different version of me that night.

I ended up explaining everything to my mother that night, as if I had any other option. I was terrified when I got to the part of me losing my virginity to him.

"So, Fallon," my mother spoke, " I've created a safe space for you to be able to come and talk to me about anything, and you mean to tell me that before you gave up something that you could never get back; you didn't talk to me about it?"

"Ma, I honestly wasn't planning it, it just happened. I wish that it didn't, but it did. I'm sorry," I told her.

"Naw, baby girl, there isn't anything to be sorry for. I just want you to know that I'm on your side and no one else's. Just remember that I am always here for you. I love you. You're my favorite daughter," Stormy replied, smiling.

"I'M YOUR ONLY DAUGHTER, and I love you too, best friend," I joked.

"Yeah okay, talking about some best friend," she said.

My mother and I shared a laugh.

Even though she didn't agree with my choice, she never made me regret telling her.

She did make me a gynecologist appointment the next day and made me get on birth control pills. She never mentioned a word of it to Fonzo. OG for the win!

Dominik called my phone all day and all night. I went on about my days without a care in the world, though. He called me so much that I ended up putting him on the blocked list. That didn't help because he would simply call me from different numbers, spewing threats.

After that night at my mother's house, however, I vowed to never speak to Dominik again. I was way too young to be dealing with that type of nonsense. At least, that was what I tried to tell myself.

I was young, fine, and free! It was nearing the end of the school year, which meant summer vacation. I was mainly looking forward to not waking up early as hell and partaking in endless shopping until the malls closed. The best part about having a father in "the business" was spending his money.

I finished out my last semester of sophomore year strong. I had, yet again, made Stormy proud by bringing in all A's. Even with the brief distraction from Dominik, I still kept school my number one priority.

CHAPTER 3

I kicked off the summer at my favorite place — the only real decent outlet mall in Northwest Indiana, The Lighthouse Mall. They had all of the top designers and trending looks. I was browsing through the Gucci store when I ran into this fine ass, tall nigga whose name I came to know as Kiyan. I mean, I literally ran into him. My one-track minded ass was looking through the racks and texting my friend, Tia, when I ran dead smack into his fine, caramel-colored ass. When I finally looked up, I felt star struck. He was just so damn cute — and tall as hell. He must've felt the same energy, because he smiled so big, I could see his mouth full of gold teeth.

Hood niggas had a way of making me want to drop my panties.

I felt compelled to speak first, so I smiled and said, "Hey." I'm laughing to myself, thinking back on that shit now; we were so corny.

He spoke back to me, replying with, "What's up, Joe?" It was his out west lingo for me. He continued on with the normal script, asking me my name and age. I told him that my name was Fallon, and he looked at me sexily and told me that my name was just as sexy as me.

Man, who was this nigga and why did my pussy start twerking at that moment? Sheesh!

We chopped it up a bit more before we exchanged numbers.

When I walked out of the mall, I felt like my whole day had been made. I was floating just thinking about the fine ass specimen named Kiyan. That was, until I got to my car and none other than Dominik was leaning up against my car.

"Dominik, what the fuck are you doing? Get your half slow ass off of my car!"

"Girl, calm your simple ass down. I just want to talk to you!"

"NIGGA, I don't want to hear shit from you! You came to my fucking house, and that shit was disrespectful as hell!" I was fuming.

"Then you should have answered the damn phone when I called. I told you that I'm not to be played with! That's my pussy, Fallon!"

"Nigga, you wish. I'm done with you! I got a new nigga now," I told him, even though I didn't really have a new man.

"Fallon, I don't give a fuck about what you think you have. That shit between your legs is mine now!"

"Nah Joe, that shit is mine now."

My neck snapped to the right superfast as I saw Kiyan nearing me and Dominik. My smile stretched extra wide, watching Kiyan walk over to me with some of his friends in my defense.

"Fallon, who the fuck is this nigga talking crazy to me?" Dominik asked.

"I told you that I had a new nigga, so, old hoe, meet my new bae!" I said.

"So, it's really like that, you goofy little bitch?" Now Dominik was fuming.

I didn't even have to respond because Kiyan pulled out his gun and pointed it in Dominik's face. Once Kiyan pulled his pistol out, his friends pulled theirs out also. I had never seen Dominik bitch up so fast! It was very entertaining, though. Dominik raised his hands in surrender and told Kiyan, "I don't want no smoke, Big Dog; I'll leave her alone."

"Good," was the only word Kiyan spoke.

I never saw or heard from Dominik after that. Kiyan never asked me any questions about him either. He told me that he would hit me up the next day, and he did.

I COULDN'T EVEN CONTAIN myself when he hit me up the next morning with a "Good Morning Beautiful" text message.

Stormy walked in the room to tell me something, and I didn't hear anything she said. I was too busy typing cute messages back and forth with Kiyan.

My mother immediately picked up on my giddiness and asked me if it was that goofy-looking little boy who came to her house unannounced.

I had to catch myself because I almost told her ass, "hell no," but I caught myself and simply told her no. Stormy wasn't stupid, though. She knew it was a boy. She left the conversation at "just be careful," and left me looking silly.

"Ma, do you really think that I would deal with someone like that after what he did?" I asked.

"Girl look, I know what kind of hold some dick can have over a young girl, trust me. I'm not about to get into that conversation with you right now, though, so like I said; be careful," she sassed.

"Ok Ma, I hear you!"

After that brief interaction, Stormy was out of the door, and I continued on with my conversation with Kiyan.

By day thirty of constant texting, shopping, movie and TV dates, I was all into Mr. Kiyan McDade. He had just made nineteen years old and graduated high school — barely. But he graduated, and that's what was important.

Kiyan was a stinking Cancer. Cancers were the worst. Most were known for being liars and for being sneaky. It was all good, though. All I knew was that I was definitely feeling him. The only thing that I didn't fully agree with in the beginning of our budding relationship, was the fact that Kiyan looked up to Fonzo and my brothers. He eventually started selling drugs.

Kiyan wasn't a Northwest Indiana native. He was from Chicago — Out west to be precise, so it was nothing new for a young boy from the hood to be in the streets. That type of lifestyle was almost expected of these young boys out here.

It just wasn't a lifestyle I desired. Fonzo and my brothers were the perfect examples of "nothing lasts forever".

I didn't fall back from Kiyan, though. We maintained a pretty good relationship, until the status he was gaining started to go to his head.

Kiyan and I spent lots of time together, whenever he wasn't making money. He even met Stormy and my Granny, who both really adored him. My relationship with Kiyan technically lasted about three years before things went downhill.

It wasn't until after I graduated that things between us went south.

At that point, Fonzo had been locked up for about two and a half years, but he still had his hands dipped in all the pots. It was as if Fonzo and his gang of soldiers were even harder to contain from the inside of a jail cell.

My mom made me go to the prison with her to show my face once I graduated high school. I still didn't understand why my mother visited my father so much. Let her tell it, she was only checking on him, but hey, it was her story to tell, mmkay? Fonzo had the biggest and brightest smile on his handsome face. I could honestly see how women let my father knock them off their square. He was fine, honey!

He couldn't maintain his signature French braids in prison, so he rocked a nice, curly ponytail.

WHEN FONZO SAW ME, he reached his arms out for a hug, and I'll admit, it was weird. First off, Fonzo never really smiled. Secondly, he called me Pooh Butt. He hadn't called me that since I was three years old.

I put on a fake smile, hoping that it would help get me through the visit. I was almost in the clear when Fonzo walked over to me, leaned in my ear, and told me to stay away from Kiyan. Whew! I felt flames rise up in my chest!

In my head, I wanted to know how the fuck could a man, who barely showed affection, love, or rarely spent any quality time with their only daughter; tell her who she could be around?

I was livid at that moment, but I knew better than to get out of pocket with him. I politely nodded my head and walked out. I kept quiet until we got in the car. I needed to know if Stormy was telling my business or not.

Once we started back home, I asked my mother if she told Fonzo about Kiyan, and she told me that she didn't and didn't even know he knew about Kiyan.

"Look Fallon, this is one of those things that you need to discuss with your father on your own. This isn't a scenario that I have to involve myself in. Talk to your dad; he's changing, and he'll listen to you," she said.

I turned my head and rolled my eyes. I wasn't foolish enough to think that Fonzo was "changing."

I did, however, believe my mother and remembered I would have been a damn fool to think that someone wouldn't tell my daddy about me seriously dating a drug dealer. Too bad Daddy Dearest was about two years too late.

I don't know what Fonzo was thinking, but I was far from done with Kiyan.

Kiyan and I dated for about six more months, until I got a private phone call from a girl stating that she and Kiyan had been dating as well. It was early in the morning on a Friday; I'll never forget it. I stayed over at Kiyan's house, and he'd just gotten up to start making his moves for the day, and my phone started ringing. I usually didn't answer private calls, but I hadn't been paying attention, and I answered before I could get a good look at the caller I.D.

Me: Hello

Unknown Caller: Yeah hello, is this Fallon?

Me: Yes, who is this?

By this time, Kiyan had picked up on my instant attitude and walked over to see what was wrong.

Unknown Caller: Oh honey, don't worry about who this is. Just

know that I've been sucking and fucking on Kiyan for a little minute now. I just thought that I would give you a courtesy call to inform you that you're on borrowed time with him.

Me: Bitch, don't call my phone with this bullshit! Either call straight through and announce yourself or get the fuck off of my line! Just know that when I catch you, ya through!

Unknown Caller: Tell that nigga to tell you what's really up before I do!

The unknown caller hung up the phone on me.

That day, after I informed my cheating ass boyfriend about the nature of the morning call. I also found out that Kiyan had a baby due in seven more months. I told Kiyan that I never wanted to see his stupid ass face again. I got up out of his bed, got my shit, and got the hell out of there.

Devastated was an understatement! I cried for weeks about that break-up. I felt like I had lost a piece of me that day. Kiyan called me day and night, trying to explain himself. He begged me to take him back, and he told me that he fucked up by letting the money and hoes get to him. Of course, I took him back like a dumb ass, but I was no longer the same with him.

Kiyan may have been sorry, and he probably never would've done it again, but the scar of a new baby coming had cut way too deep.

The day I received Terica's phone call constantly replayed in my head.

I later found out that Fonzo caught wind of Kiyan's double-life and wanted to spare me. I couldn't even be mad at Fonzo for trying to warn me. When he saw that I wasn't going to take his warning for face value, he decided to let me be a big girl and handle it myself.

My thoughts got so bad regarding what I should do, that I started purposely flirting with his opps in the hood. When hanging out with my friends, we would even hit up the spots where Kiyan would kick it out west, just so I could get a little attention from the guys out there. I started caring less and less about a relationship and more about hanging out.

Kiyan noticed and constantly asked me if I was ok. I would tell him that I was fine, but the truth was that his daughter's due date was quickly approaching, and I was the opposite of fine.

"Fal, you'll let me know if we weren't good, right?" he asked.

"Yes Kiyan, damn!" was my reply.

"Aight Joe, I'm just checking. You know you're my baby."

"Naw, I don't know anything."

"Come on, Fal," he sighed.

"Ain't no damn 'come on, Fal!'"

This was a common conversation between Kiyan and me. I was drained emotionally.

KIYAN TRIED his best to make things right with me. I mean, that boy did every single thing he could think of to try and make me feel secure about the situation. He even wanted me with him more, so he started coming in early from the block.

The more Kiyan tried, the closer to the door I got. One smart thing I did was continue living with my mother. I felt that if I had moved in with Kiyan, I would've been obligated to stay in a relationship with him.

I felt bad for the different things I took Kiyan through, but you know what they say about a woman scorned. I started cheating just because I could. Who did he think he was to even cheat on a bad bitch like me anyway? With a broad who couldn't compare to me on my worst day.

I started messing with a boy from one of the blocks that Kiyan kicked it on. I knew Jay and Kiyan weren't cool, but I honestly didn't know that they wanted one another dead.

It wasn't until I started having burning sensations when I used the restroom and went to the doctor for an emergency STD test that I found out just how deep it was about to get.

I had snuck around with Jay from time to time, whenever I got bored. It just so happened that the last time we had sex, the condom broke. I had been on birth control since I lost my virginity, so pregnancy wasn't my main concern. The day of my doctor's appointment,

I found out two things — one, that I was indeed pregnant and two, I had contracted Chlamydia. I was LIVID!! I was literally ready to kill someone! At that moment, I realized I needed to ask myself, "Fallon, who the fuck IS responsible for this mess?"

I knew that I had gotten myself into some shit. How did I end up pregnant and with an STD? Good job, Fallon. The first thing I had to do was figure out exactly how long I'd been pregnant and by whom. That was the easy part because my doctor informed me that I was four months pregnant. The slip up with Jay happened three weeks prior to my appointment, so I was in the clear for that part.

The STD, on the other hand, was completely up in the air. I honestly couldn't pinpoint who gave me the damn disease. I had a strange feeling that made me know Kiyan hadn't burned me. I truly felt like he was doing right by me, but the damage was already done. I wasn't a grimy bitch, so I definitely had to have a sit down with Kiyan and tell him the truth about what was going on. As far as Jay's hoe ass, I had to leave his dirty dick ass alone!

Kiyan's baby was due in any day and there I was, sitting there looking dumb while being four months pregnant AND burning. What was my life amounting to? I really was clueless out here!

The day came when I had to finally tell Kiyan what had transpired with Jay. I was nervous as hell when I walked through the door of his apartment while he sat there, looking full of concern. I didn't know exactly where to begin, so I just started from the beginning. "Kiyan, I haven't been happy, which led me to cheat on you," I blurted out. He looked so hurt. I literally saw the sadness, amongst other emotions, on his contorted face.

"Damn Joe, tell me how you really feel," he stated sarcastically.

"I'm serious, Kiyan. It's fucked up, and I apologize, but that's my truth."

"I guess I kind of knew that something was wrong, but I didn't expect this," he said.

"That's not it though. There are a few more things that you should know."

He didn't know what to say or do, so I continued with the rest of the story.

THERE WAS a twinge in Kiyan's face when I told him how I had been having sex with Jay. His nice, peanut butter complexion turned crimson. Kiyan was heated, and I felt that heat radiate off of him from where I stood in a corner of the room. He looked as if he was trying to compose himself, and I made a mental note to keep my distance. Kiyan got up and walked to the kitchen. His movements were quiet, and I never moved an inch. When he came back into the room, there was a drink in a whiskey glass, and I knew that it had to be either Peach or Apple Crown Royal. Kiyan sat back down in his seat and said, "Continue."

That's just what I did, too.

By the time I told Kiyan every single detail, I knew that he felt everything I felt a few months prior. He wanted to know all of the details pertaining to my fling with Jay, so I told him. He asked me questions about where we would meet up and how often we had sex. I wasn't trying to stick the knife in further, but I guess he felt that he needed to know. Kiyan stood up a few more times, paced back and forth, and yelled out "fuck," at least a dozen times.

The next thing that came out of Kiyan's mouth made me feel like maybe I had fucked up royally.

"I don't know why you want to play these games with me, Joe, but you just got this nigga killed!"

"Kiyan, just relax for a second! I did this! I'm the one who cheated on you! I'm the one who isn't happy! You need to deal with me, not him!"

"Fallon, you heard what I said! We gon' be good, but I'm at that nigga head!" he said as he walked out of the room.

My little confession started a whole street war. Kiyan was out for blood, and there wasn't a thing I could do about it. He wanted Jay's head on a platter.

Kiyan was mad at me, that much I could tell, but he never spoke on the situation again. It wasn't my intention to admit my wrongs to him for us to makeup and pretend like everything was ok between us. I told the truth because everyone involved was affected by my decisions.

The birth of Kiyan's baby girl came faster than I expected. I cried. I felt like I died. I also made a decision that day. I knew that no matter the cost or where I had to go, I wasn't keeping the baby that was growing inside of me. I began the search of finding a clinic to go to because I needed an abortion and fast. It may have been out of hurt or anger — maybe even resentment towards Kiyan, but I couldn't go through with having a baby.

Once I broke the news to Kiyan, he threw a fit!

"Why the fuck would you kill my seed, Joe?" Kiyan was pissed.

"I don't want to have this baby, Kiyan, damn!"

"You don't want to have a baby or MY baby?"

"Both!" I yelled.

"Fuck you, Fallon! You're being selfish as fuck, Joe! What the fuck is wrong with you? You'd kill our seed because you're mad at me?"

"Yes, Kiyan. That's exactly what I'm doing."

The fucking nerve of this nigga! How was it that he had a whole newborn that he had to take care of but got mad at me because I wasn't about to give birth to his second child in the same year? I think the fuck not! That day, we argued for well over two hours, and the outcome remained the same. I was set to get the procedure done the next week.

Kiyan stormed out, and I couldn't have been any more unbothered by it than I was at that moment.

Kiyan hadn't spoken to me in the days leading up to the procedure, and that suited me just fine. I thought I was a tough bitch walking in that clinic, but to my dismay, I was the total opposite. Seeing all of those girls sitting there looking scared and lonely made my chest tighten up. I realized in that moment that I was scared and lonely my damn self.

I called Kiyan's phone, and he sent me to voicemail. I called once more, and he picked up with an attitude.

"Yeah man?!" he answered in an irritated tone.

"Kiyannnnnnn." I dragged his name out purposely.

All I had to do was say his name once. He heard the frightened tone in my voice and immediately asked "What's wrong, Fal? Where are you?"

I told him that I was at the clinic, and he was there by my side ten minutes later. I could tell that he was uncomfortable being there, but it's what I needed to do for me, so he endured it.

I can't lie and say that the whole process wasn't traumatic, because it was, but I just couldn't see myself being a baby mama at that point in my life.

We walked out of the clinic that day hand in hand.

"Are you sure that you're okay, Fallon? Do you need anything?" he asked.

"No, I'm just ready to go home and get some rest," I told him solemnly.

"Well, for the record, you know that I am just a phone call away."

"Yeah, I know," I told him, but I believe we both knew that the dynamic of our relationship had changed.

As the days went on, I healed physically, but mentally and emotionally, I was damaged. I should've talked to someone — a therapist, my mother; hell, or even Fonzo.

I was all over the place, trying to figure out what was next. Kiyan reached out on several occasions, and we spent a little time together, but my heart just wasn't in it anymore.

I noticed a change in him as well. Normally, Kiyan would make me feel through his words and actions that even though the streets needed him, I was a priority, even though I was being a total bitch towards him. I would have his undivided attention. Those days in particular, he barely even gave me eye contact. I tried addressing it, but he would insist that I was tripping. I would even try to kick off a conversation with him. "Kiyan, what's up? You good? I'm not used to you being so quiet."

"I'm good, Joe. I gotta get to this money. I'll hit you up later," and then he'd be gone.

I was completely cool on him for real after that.

Once I was fully healed, I resumed going back outside with Tia. She was my go-to if I wanted to be in the streets. That's probably one of main reasons Kiyan didn't really care for us going out together. Oh well.

I called my girl and per usual, she answered and was excited to hear from me.

"Hey bitchhhhhh!" she sang into the phone.

"Heyy best friend! What's the tea, bitch? What's cracking tonight?" I asked.

"Girl, are you sure about going out? You need to be healing," she asked me genuinely concerned.

"Bitch, I'm fine. I'm ready to get out here in the streets and cut up!" I told her.

"Well, say less then. Pick me up at ten o'clock. I'm sure that between the two of us, we'll figure something out."

"Okay girl, I'll see you then," I told her, and then we hung up.

THAT NIGHT, we went joy riding and ended up at Club Wiggles. Wiggles was a popular strip club located in Hammond, Indiana. The bouncers in the club never gave us any problems letting our underage asses in because they knew Fonzo and The Boys. Tia and I were having a good time, sipping our drinks when a brown-skinned cutie approached me, asking for my name. Of course, I played hard to get because, well shit, my name is Fallon motherfucking Jax!

"What's good, Lil Mama, what's your name?" Brown-skinned asked me.

I told his ass, "Nun-ya," while turning my back to him.

"Well, Miss Nun-ya, when are you going to let a nigga like me kiss on those pretty lips?"

I faced him and gave him attitude as I licked my lips, which were popping with my matte-stained lip gloss from Couth Cosmetics. I then told him in the sexiest voice that I could muster, "Get in line, Daddy," turning my back on his ass yet again.

Cutie pie must've thought I was playing because he continued to run game like he just knew I was interested. He wasn't even fazed by me "attempting" to play him for a sucker.

The mystery man was oh so fine, though. He was muscular and had a head full of waves that made me sea-sick just looking at them. His next statement made my knees weak when he said, "Just so you know, you licked the wrong set of lips. I was referring to the ones below your sexy ass waistline."

It took a lot out of my thot ass, but I held my ground, and I told his ass I was good and turned my back on him yet again. One would think that any man that had been rejected repeatedly would move on to the next, but not this nigga. I would've never expected him to walk around, face me, grab me by the chin, and kiss me on the forehead. A forehead kiss! Why did he make me cream my panties like that, man? I didn't know whether I wanted to fuck this nigga or fight him!

Unfortunately, that forehead kiss was the beginning of some straight up bullshit.

UNTITLED

Mr. Brown-skinned cutie, whose name was Torrance Bridges, was the beginning of the end of my sanity. That man did everything in the world he could to bring me down. When I'm alone with my thoughts, one of the few regrets I have in life was meeting Torrance. The night me and Tia left Wiggles, me and Torrance exchanged numbers. He was so persistent on top of being sexy, it seemed like the only logical thing to do was see what his fine ass would bring my way. That intimate ass forehead kiss was just the cherry on top.

* * *

I ended up back at Kiyan's house because it was a shorter drive from having to drop Tia off at her house. I was drunk, but I still didn't get the urge to give Kiyan any play. I was still bothered by him and the fact that he had a bitch calling his phone randomly about what Kiyari, the baby, needed. Terica found a reason to dial Kiyan's number every single day. Some days the delusional bitch would call just to say, "Kiyari misses her daddy." I was completely outdone the day Terica's crazy ass called to say, "Kiyan, the baby is trying to talk already. She said, "DaDa." She knew damn well that a damn newborn was barely even awake long enough to say anything, let alone "Dada!" Kiyan didn't allow Terica to get under his skin, but she for damn sure got under mine.

Kiyan looked like he had something heavy on his mind anyway, so I took that as my cue to get in the shower and go to bed.

Kiyan stopped me as I tried to make a beeline to the bathroom. "Hold up, Fal, can I holler at you for a minute?"

"Kiyan, I'm kind of tired right now. Plus, I've been drinking, so I'm ready to call it a night."

"Aight then, Joe."

I almost felt bad, because Kiyan spoke as if he was defeated. That was another conversation for a different day, so I continued on to the bathroom.

While in the shower, the combination of the hot water and liquor had me going. I was kind of shocked when I started touching myself to the thoughts of "Mr. Brown-Skinned Forehead Kisser." There was something about that man's aura. I got wet just thinking about him.

Once I got out of the shower and dried off, I walked to Kiyan's closet to grab a T-shirt. Kiyan grabbed me by the hand.

"Fallon, just know that everything is going to get better. I'm going to fix all of this shit between us."

Oh, how I wished that it was that easy. I really wish that I would've known then that Kiyan loved me the most. Maybe I would've tried harder in our relationship. I simply responded with an "ok" and walked off.

That night, Kiyan said something else that I didn't quite understand at the time, but I get it now.

He said, "Fal, I know that you think that you're running out of maybes and losing a little patience; but I'm the one who really loves you, Joe. I am always going to be your home.

I didn't have any smart replies or comebacks so I got in the bed, with Kiyan following suit. It took me no time before I drifted off to sleep. Kiyan's words had replayed over and over in my head however.

The next morning, when I looked at my phone, I saw text messages from Torrance:

Forehead Kisser: Good Morning Beautiful.

Me: Hey, good morning.

Forehead Kisser: How are you feeling, Queen?

Me: I'm great, how about you?

Forehead Kisser: I can't call it, Ma. I'm blessed. I can't stop thinking about you, beautiful.

Either I was a girly girl or just foolish, but that kind of stuff used to win me over fast.

I always felt like *damn, he's thinking of me* or *I've got to be so lucky to have a nigga who seems to be a big deal reaching out to ME first thing in the morning*. While that may be true for some, it isn't true for all, and that's on Mary Had a Little Lamb, mmkay?

See, Torrance had plans for me. I just didn't know what they were. He made me feel like I was the luckiest girl in the world. Torrance gave me a distraction from whatever weird space Kiyan and I were in. It was as if I was becoming more and more disengaged from Kiyan, and Torrance started requesting to be in my presence more frequently. He would look me in my eyes and say things like, "Fallon, I need your fine ass with me every day."

My weak ass always fell for it — hook, line and sinker too.

I never wanted to miss an opportunity to be around him either, but I still tried not to throw anything in Kiyan's face.

It seemed like the sneaking I did with Torrance was worth it at the time, but he wanted me to feel that way so that I would become comfortable with him.

* * *

While I was off in la-la land with Torrance, word got back to me that the feud between Kiyan and Jay had gotten worse throughout the weeks.

Jay ended up trying to get to Kiyan at the strip club one night. I was told that Jay and his crew attempted to walk into the strip club with guns on them and were stopped by the club security. There was an argument at the door that caught Kiyan's attention, so he got up to see what was going on. Unbeknownst to Jay, Kiyan held part ownership of the strip club; so, he and whoever he was with were never searched. When Kiyan walked to the door and saw who was causing the chaos, he started laughing at Jay's troubles, which only added fuel to Jay's burning rage. Jay pulled out his gun, prompting his crew to do the same. In turn, Kiyan and his goons followed suit. The story got conflicted because some people say that Kiyan fired the first shot, and some people say that it was Jay. Either way, one of the bouncers was killed and a few others were injured. When the police arrived, no one was willing to go against Kiyan, so that led to Jay and his people being arrested.

Jay ended up being charged with the bouncer's death and another body, which led to him being sentenced to sixty-five years in prison.

I can't say that I was sad to see him go out like that, but it's also not something that I would wish on anybody.

* * *

Whenever I would have a bad day or just needed to vent, I would call Torrance. He was so easy to talk to. The day that I heard about what went down between Kiyan and Jay, I called Torrance to lightly vent about it. He answered on the first ring.

"Hey Beautiful, what's up with you?" he asked.

"Shit, I just found out that some crazy shit happened between you know who and another nigga I know."

"Shit like what?" Torrance asked, completely engulfed in what I was talking about.

"Nothing really, just some stupid shit that led to people being badly hurt and even dying."

"Damn baby, are you cool?" Do you need me to come wherever you are?" Tell Daddy what you need."

"No boo, I'm okay. I just needed to get that off of my chest," I assured him.

"Alright, well you know where I'm at if you need me."

"Yes, I do." I smiled.

"Okay bae, I got some shit to handle, so hit me up later," he said.

"Okay, bye." I was smiling from ear to ear at this point.

Torrance had me feeling like I could tell him just about anything. He made me feel like I didn't have to hide anything from him. I was falling in love with my little side dip. After a while, I started wanting to be around Torrance only.

* * *

Kiyan ended up figuring out that my attention was elsewhere. He approached me one day and asked what I had going on. Kiyan was insistent that I tell him who I was fucking with. I got so tired of the back and forth that I said to that nigga, "Hell the fuck yes! I WILL DO WHAT THE FUCK I WANT TO DO WITH MY PUSSY!" I told that nigga that if HE didn't like it then HE could move the fuck around.

"Fallon, you are not going to keep fucking playing with me like I'm some lil' nigga out here!"

"I'm not treating you like a lil' nigga! I'm treating you like I'm over all of this shit!"

"Over what, Fallon? A nigga who's trying to love your spoiled ass the right way? All I have been doing is trying to make shit right, Joe, but you don't appreciate SHIT!" He stressed that last part.

"Kiyan, I'm just tired at this point. Tired of talking, tired of arguing, tired of all of it," I told him.

I was so tired of even pretending anymore. Kiyan was going to stay or go, but I wasn't going to stop messing with Torrance. Kiyan didn't know it, but I really meant it.

"What changed you, man? I don't want a bullshit answer either, tell me what's up."

I cannot believe that he just looked me in the face and asked what changed me. I scoffed as I looked Kiyan in his face and told him the complete truth about what exactly made me feel the way I felt.

"Kiyan, you fucking cheated and Kiyari is the consequence. It's too much for me to handle."

"Bae, Kiyari and her mother are permanent fixtures in our world. I'm sorry about that, but I want to move past the bad shit with you by my side." Kiyan told me what I already knew.

I knew that was the reality, but I was not ok with it.

Kiyan took my lingering silence as a sign of good faith, I'm assuming, because he asked if we were good as if anything had been resolved. I was done with the entire conversation at that point, so I simply told him yes just to leave it alone. I guess he took that response and ran with it like somehow things were fixed between us and took a phone call that required him to leave. I was fine with that because I took that as an opportunity to go see Torrance.

I called him, and he picked up on the first ring.

"Hey sexy." Torrance spoke into the phone with that deep baritone voice that turned me on.

"Hey boo, I'm on my way outside. Do you have a little time for me today?"

"I always have time for your pretty ass."

"Is that right?" By this time, there was a puddle in between my legs.

"Hell yeah. Pull up on me, baby!"

"Okay, send me the address, and I'll be on my way," I told him.

"Bet," Torrance replied, and we hung the phone up.

The smile on my face was one mile long. Torrance really knew exactly what to say to get my juices down below flowing.

CHAPTER 4

I met up with Torrance at a local bar called Coaches Corner. I wasn't quite of legal age to be there, but the bouncers there knew me and who my family was, so they never gave me problems about getting in. When Torrance walked in, I noticed that he gave dap to the bouncers and acknowledged the staff, which let me know that he must've frequented the bar. He walked up to me, smelling so damn good that I wanted to fuck him right on top of the bar. I had to slow myself down before I got in some trouble. Torrance hugged me and sat down next to me at the bar. He asked, "What are you drinking?"

"I think I'll take a watermelon Long Island iced tea."

"Okay," he said and then ordered a double shot of peach Crown for himself.

The bartender gave us our drinks, and I started vibing to the music that was playing when Torrance turned completely around in his seat and laid some heavy shit on me. He began with, "Fallon, I'm not none of these little niggas you're used to playing with."

I was super confused, partially because of the effects of the liquor. All I could do was giggle as I asked, "What are you talking about?"

Torrance glared at me with a serious face and asked, "Fallon, do you think that I am a joke? You think that what I'm saying is a game?"

At that point, I had to sober up a bit because I didn't want to look foolish if he was being serious. I responded with, "No boo, I don't think that you're any of those things. I just need you to elaborate."

I guess he liked that reply better because he continued on. "Baby, I want you all to myself. You need to leave that weak ass nigga alone."

I don't know exactly what I was expecting or what I was looking to come from dealing with Torrance, but I do know that this conversation was never something that I thought would come up.

I looked at Torrance, and by this time, I was completely sobering up.

"Torrance, I can't just up and leave Kiyan. Where is all of this coming from?"

"Where is this coming from?" he repeated.

"Yes, that's what I asked. I thought we were good like we are baby, what's wrong?" I needed to diffuse this situation quickly.

"Fallon, you can leave him, if that's what you really wanted to do. It's not that damn hard; you aren't married to his ass."

"I understand what you're saying, boo. Just give me a little time, and I'll do it."

He continued ranting, "I feel like you're wasting my time, Fallon. I am a grown ass man, and I don't have time for childish games."

"How am I wasting your time? I'm here with you right now. Why doesn't that count?"

What I quickly learned about men is that sometimes, you have to stroke their egos a bit, just to get things on track.

"Yeah, it counts," he answered. "But if you were mine, you would always be with me."

By this time, I ordered myself another drink because the conversation was way too much.

Once my drink arrived, I waited until Torrance was done talking before I hit him with, "we haven't even had sex yet and you want me to just leave my boyfriend for you?"

I guess what I said was the joke of the year because Torrance laughed at me. I mean, one of the infectious laughs that made me want to chuckle too. I, however, didn't see a damn thing funny.

Torrance looked at me with a straight face and said, "Fallon, I haven't put this dick in you yet out of the best interest of you. I've been sparing you, love."

I scoffed at him and asked, "What do you mean by that?"

"Baby, if I put this dick in you, I'll break that little pussy in half." He smirked.

I took great offense to that statement, but my half slow ass was also turned the hell on. I didn't even have any comebacks or rebuttals. All I could do was sip my drink and half ass reply, "stop playing with me." That's it. That's all I had. Torrance knew what the hell he was doing to me. He had a PhD in mind-fucking me. I hated the fact that he was sitting right in front of me, grinning like he knew something I didn't. The smile was a taunting one, and the direct eye contact was making me want to do some very freaky things to him in a public place, not even caring about it being crowded. I had to check myself, fast.

I downed my drink and told Torrance that I needed to get back home.

"Are you ok?" he asked.

"Yes, I'm fine. I'm getting tired," I lied.

Torrance laughed and said, "Yeah, okay."

He closed out the tab and walked me to my car. Just as we approached the car, I got a late-night phone call from my mother. Stormy never called late, so I immediately answered. "Hey Ma, is everything alright?" I asked full of concern.

"Yes baby, I'm fine. I just wanted to check up on you. The last few times you were home, we missed one another. I'm worried about you, and I miss my baby."

"Aww, thanks, Mommy, but I'm good. I've just been hanging out," I told her.

"Hanging out. Okay baby girl, well, when you get some free time, I want to see you. We need to talk."

My mother could literally read me like a book, so she must've known that I was on some bullshit that night.

"Ok Ma, I hear you. I promise you one day over the weekend, I will come sit with you, watch some of our favorite movies and have some girl talk. She bought that, and we got off of the phone.

Torrance was leaning on my car, watching me on the phone while looking sexy as hell doing so. I smiled and asked, "Why are you staring at me?"

He walked over to me while licking his lips. When we were finally face to face, he grabbed me by my neck and gave me his whole damn tongue. I'm talking about the "crème de la crème" of French kisses.

Torrance whispered in my ear and said, "Give me this pussy." His tone was so masculine, and the bass in his voice, along with the liquor pulsing through my veins, had me tingling inside.

We immediately started tearing at each other's clothes right in the parking lot. Now, I was a wild girl, but I had never done anything that wild in my life! He pulled my Fendi skirt down to my ankles, lifted me up, and pulled all of what had to be at least ten inches of dick inside of me. I couldn't breathe when he entered me.

Lord, why would you give one man good looks, money, and a dick this damn big? That had to be what devil dick was. I couldn't take it. I tried to get off of his ass, but he held on to me tighter.

That nigga had the nerve to say, "Take that dick and stop running!"

Nigga, I can't! You're knocking my uterus out of place! That's what I wanted to say, but I couldn't get a word out.

I wanted to yell, kick, scream, and get that nigga off of me, but then it started feeling so damn good. It began to feel way too good, so I started doing circles on the D in mid-air while grinding back on him. "Oh my God, Torrance! Fuck me!" I moaned. I really started to show out when I felt him about to cum. I started licking and biting his neck while humping him as hard as my spine would allow. He just couldn't let me be great, though, and decided to show me who was really in charge. "Yeah," he said as he pounded me.

"This dick is good, huh? Stop running! TAKE. THIS. DICK!"

"Torrance! Okay, okay okay! Damn, this is good!" My mind was blown away.

Kiyan wasn't no little dick nigga, but Torrance had girth and length on him, so he was hitting spots I didn't even know that I had.

Torrance fucked me for at least five more minutes until he finally put me down and came hard as hell in his hand. We were both so caught up, that we didn't even think about a condom. I couldn't play myself a second time around, though, and I asked him straight out, "Look, do I need to go get tested?"

"We're good on my end, Ma. Are you on birth control?"

"Yes, but I'll still go and get a Plan B in the morning."

"Okay Ma, you good? I told you that I would murder that pussy."

"Yeah, but I really need to get back, especially since it's almost two in the morning."

Torrance's facial expression told me that he didn't like what I'd told him, though and decided to remind me of our previous conversation. "Fallon, don't forget what I told you. I want you to be mine. I own that pussy now, so don't make me wait long."

"Okay Torr, I got you. You have to be patient with me, boo, and just give me some time." I gave him a kiss, got in my car, and pulled off.

When I drove off, I looked in my rearview mirror. I saw Torrance literally watching me. It was so strange because I could have sworn he was smiling. I didn't pay it too much attention though, so I immediately pulled out my phone and called Tia. I had to let my girl know everything that happened that night.

CHAPTER 5

Tia couldn't believe the story I told her about how I busted it open for Torrance's fine ass in the middle of a parking lot. I couldn't believe myself either. It had become awkwardly quiet in the room once I finished telling her everything.

"Bitch, I cannot believe you!" Tia exclaimed.

"I know girl, me either. He just made me feel carefree!"

Tia looked me square in the eyes and asked, "But what are you really doing with Torrance? You got that man talking about being serious and you leaving Kiyan."

"I don't know, honestly. All I know is that I'm digging the hell out of Torrance. Kiyan is becoming a faded memory."

"Girl please, Kiyan is not letting you go easily, so you had better come up with a plan."

"I know, friend. I know."

* * *

My twentieth birthday was quickly approaching, and I had major plans. I didn't want to go completely crazy until my twenty-first birthday, but I wasn't going to not turn all the way up for twenty.

Every year since I could remember, my mother would take me on spa and dinner dates for my birthday, followed by a big birthday party. Fonzo and my mother would also present me with lavish gifts on my birthdays. This particular year, I didn't mind keeping the tradition, however, I had plans of throwing my own bash — a more grown version.

"WHAT DO you want for your birthday, Fal?" Kiyan asked.

"I don't really know; just surprise me, I guess."

Kiyan repeatedly asked me what I wanted for my birthday every year since we'd been together, and I'd always hit him with "I don't know." I never knew. I did, however, know exactly what I wanted this year. What Kiyan didn't know was that I wanted something special from someone else.

May ninth rolled around quickly, and I was over ready! I had my hair, nails, and feet slayed the day before, so the only thing I needed to do before my party was get my makeup and lashes done.

Torrance had been texting me throughout the day, every day. Most of our threads consisted of the things he normally texted, like the "hey beautiful" messages. However, our threads also consisted of messages that made me nervous, like the texts that read, "So when are you leaving that nigga?" I would just blow it off and tell him to give me some more time. I could tell that he was growing impatient, though.

The spa appointment that my mother scheduled for us was amazing! I'd gotten the most intense, deep massage that I'd ever received. The spa we went to offered mimosas, so my mother worked her magic and got me out of having to show I.D. While we were drinking and relaxing, Stormy decided to start up a conversation with me. "So Diva, what's new with you?"

"Nothing really. I've been staying under the radar."

"Under the radar, huh?" Stormy scoffed.

"What is that supposed to mean, Ma?"

. . .

"YOU AND KIYAN used to be joined at the hip. I haven't seen much of that lately."

What started off as small talk, turned into Stormy trying to figure me out.

"Kiyan has just been busy." I shrugged.

Stormy knew I was lying. One thing about Stormy Swilley is that she could read me like a book. "Umm hmm, well you and Kiyan need to start making time for each other. You also have to stop acting disinterested in him, Fallon. I see shit too, you know."

"Come on, Ma, can we enjoy the spa please?"

I guess Stormy caught the hint that not only was I disinterested in Kiyan, but I was also disinterested in the conversation at hand.

She looked me in my eyes, which mimicked hers and said to me, "Fallon, whatever the fuck you're doing in these streets, you'd better stop it."

She continued, "I can't tell you how to live your life, you're grown now, but you are playing dangerously if you're doing what I think you are."

I wanted to ask her what she had been referring to, but I really wanted to be done with the conversation.

"I don't know what you're talking about. I'm not doing anything."

My mom shook her head and turned away from me. I felt bad because I wanted to be able to tell my mother everything, but I knew that she wouldn't understand.

Once I was done spending time with my mother, I went back to Kiyan's house to get dressed for the night. Kiyan was, of course, accompanying me for the night to my party. Hell, he was the one paying for it.

CHAPTER 6

When Kiyan and I arrived at my party's venue, I walked in and was in awe. I couldn't believe that everything I envisioned came to life the way it did. Everything looked amazing. The Coco Chanel theme that I told the planner I wanted was to die for! There were black double C's all over the place, complemented with pink Eiffel Towers. Judy, the party planner, had earned every penny of Kiyan's money. There was a gift table to my left that was already filled to capacity. When I walked over to see who the gifts were from, I was shocked to see Fonzo and my brothers' names on several of the boxes. Some big and some small. It was a bit of a surprise that The Boys showed out the way that they did, because they hardly ever remembered my birthday. I'm sure Fonzo was the reason behind them remembering this year.

Fonzo however, never lacked in the gift department. It was no surprise that he'd have some things sent to me. I could tell that he wanted to be a better father to me, and I wasn't opposed to the sudden change. I figured that my mother was behind the "new leaf" that Fonzo was turning over when it was pertaining to me.

Once I snapped out of my thoughts, I walked over to Tia and a couple more girls I recognized from around the way so that I could greet my guests. The girls were hyping me up on how good I looked, and I soaked it all in.

I noticed Tia being a little shady, so I asked, "What's up with you?"

"Nothing is up. I'm just worried about you," she replied sincerely.

"Girl, relax. Go have a drink. I'm good, it's my birthdayyy!" I screamed to get the vibe back on track.

I couldn't allow myself to become annoyed on my birthday of all days. Plus, I was fine, and I didn't need everybody acting like I was making a whole bunch of bad mistakes. Shit, it was my birthday and I was young as hell, living my best life. What could be so wrong with that?

I walked to the bar and told the bartender to pour me my first drink of the night. I opted for Patrón and told the friendly face behind the bar to keep them coming. While I waited for her to finish with my drink, I felt my phone go off.

When I looked at my phone, I saw multiple text messages from Torrance. I rolled my eyes because I told him that I would hit him up the next day. I didn't tell him that for any reason other than that I wanted to enjoy my birthday party in peace, and I knew that I would be a drunk fool. I was about to be way too drunk to baby Torrance tonight. Torrance didn't see it my way though; he felt like he should have been the one celebrating with me and not Kiyan. I tried to convince him that the only reason I was there with Kiyan was because he paid for the party. Torrance didn't give two fucks about what I was talking about.

He started sending back-to-back messages.

T: Fallon, you better be at my door when the party ends, or I'm coming to get you.

I can't lie and say that I wasn't becoming a little scared of Torrance. He was aggressive and impatient. The first trait can sometimes be a turn on but combined with the latter, it was no good.

I rolled my eyes as I texted him back.

Me: Are you okay? Is there something going on? Do you need to talk?

All I saw was the three dots dancing across my iPhone screen before he replied.

T: You're right Bae, I'm tripping. Just come over to my spot tomorrow once you wake up. I have something special planned for you.

Me: Okay.

Now that brought the smile back to my face! Just like that, I was back in party mode. The remainder of my night went without incident. It wasn't until the end of the night that things went a little sideways. Kiyan had been extremely attentive to me and my needs that night. He made sure that I had a full stomach and that I kept a full cup in my hand.

It was time for me to open my gifts so that things could get wrapped up for the night. I instantly became nervous when Kiyan grabbed a microphone to make a toast. Kiyan never made public announcements. What the fuck was happening? Maybe it was the liquor, but it seemed like he was nervous as well. I continued listening and then I became hot — like the burning up hot sensation you feel before you faint.

"Fal, you are the first person I've experienced real love with. You introduced me to what courting a girl is like. Your mother is also a first experience for me. Ms. Stormy showed me what it's like having a positive mother figure, since my own mother just never cared to be a real mother to me. She was more concerned about where her next high was going to come from."

Stormy ate that up!

"Fallon, you are the only person who has the power to take me out of character. I'm a real ass gangsta in the streets, shit, grown ass men fear me; but when it comes to you, I put that shit to the side."

The entire crowd hung on to Kiyan's every word. Everyone except me.

If it had been a different time or circumstance, I would have held on to every word that came out of Kiyan's mouth as well. However, it wasn't that time or that circumstance. I had become emotionally unavailable to Kiyan.

Then, Kiyan dropped down to his left knee and pulled out the biggest, shiniest, princess-cut diamond engagement ring that I'd ever laid eyes on. I looked over to my mother and Granny, and I saw the happiness in their eyes. Then I looked over at Tia, my best damn friend, and saw the same shock in her eyes that I'm sure was written all over my face. I finally looked down at Kiyan, and instantly I started crying. I didn't cry because I was happy and ready to marry him. I cried because I could think of one hundred emotions at the time, but happiness and love weren't any of them. What I didn't want to do was embarrass Kiyan or let my mom down, so I reluctantly accepted his proposal. The smile that was on Kiyan's face would be etched in my brain for the rest of my life.

Kiyan stood and kissed me, and because there were so many people recording the moment, I kissed him back. Stormy rushed up to me first, hugging and congratulating us. She was so happy.

"Oh my God, baby! We have to start making plans immediately."

"I know, Ma! This has been some kind of day, right?" I faked the excitement the best way I could.

The only thing on my mind at that moment was, *what the hell did I just do?*

CHAPTER 7

By the time everyone got a chance to get pictures with me and Kiyan, there was no more time to finish my gift opening. It was time to pack everything up and go. Everybody started bidding their farewells, including Tia.

"I'm happy for you, friend! Call me in the morning," she said.

"Ok, you know I am."

I assured her that I would call. I, however, was not ready to be alone with my new fiancé. It didn't even sit right in my brain that I had agreed to marry Kiyan. It wasn't that I didn't love him, but I was not in love with him the same way I used to be. The damage had already been done, and too much hurt was still lingering in me. It didn't matter how many different ways Kiyan spun it, the fact that he created a life while in a relationship with me was unforgivable.

Yeah, it might've been toxic for me to pretend that we could move forward in our relationship as if things were good when they weren't, but I just didn't really care.

Everything had been put in the car, and we were all preparing to leave when my mother and my granny approached me.

"I still cannot believe that Kiyan proposed tonight!" my mother said excitedly.

"Me either. I'm really happy and excited that we're about to start planning a wedding!" said my granny.

I had to refrain from rolling my eyes, but I put on my best smile and happy face.

"I can't wait either," I told them both.

"Ooh Fal, we need to go see Fonzo and tell him the good news!" Stormy said out of the blue.

Out of the corner of my eye, I saw my granny roll her eyes at that comment. I chuckled to myself because Granny never really cared for Fonzo.

"Okay Ma, set the visit up." I agreed with my mother so that they could get going. They both kissed me goodnight, and then they left so that my mom could drop my granny off at home.

Of course, before they could get out of the door, Kiyan jogged up and insisted on walking them to the car. Stormy could've won an Oscar at that point with all of the "that's my son" comments. That right there made me have the bartender pour me one more drink for the road.

Once my mom and granny were gone, Kiyan walked up to me and asked, "Hey sexy, are you ready to go?"

I wanted to say, "hell no," but I opted for a simple "sure" instead.

Kiyan complimented me the whole ride to his house.

"You looked really sexy in that dress tonight."

"Thank you," I said politely.

"That ass was looking real fat tonight too, Joe. I can't wait to grab on to it later."

"I'm a little tired now, Kiyan."

"Maybe you'll feel better when we make it back to the crib."

"I doubt it."

It seemed like we made it to Kiyan's house in record time.

I thought that I'd be able to take off my clothes, take a nice hot shower, and go to bed.

NOT! Kiyan had plans of his own. Once we got in the house, Kiyan started pulling my clothes off.

"Bae, I've been waiting to suck on that pussy all night!"

I was not in the mood though; I really just wanted to go to sleep.

"Come on, Ki, I need some sleep," I whined.

"You can go to sleep after you cum for Daddy."

When Kiyan got me completely naked and realized that I wasn't wearing any panties, he went nuts.

"See baby, you knew what you were doing this whole time! You're not even wearing panties."

He pushed me up against the wall and threw my leg over his shoulder. He started eating me like I was The Last Supper! That was a little new to me because while Kiyan didn't have bad dick, he still never really went all out and nasty with it. He was too hood, I guess. Wild sometimes, yes, but nasty? Not so much.

CHAPTER 8

I started to get into the way he had been sloppily eating my pussy, so I began grinding his face. I don't know if Kiyan had one too many drinks that night, but for the first time in a while, I hadn't looked at him sideways. I fucked his face hard, and he thoroughly enjoyed himself. I started to feel myself cum, and he licked, sucked, and stuck his tongue in my wet slit until I finally yelled out, "Kiyan, I'm fucking cumming!" He didn't stop, though; he continued while cheering me on until I squirted my juices all in his face. Kiyan clearly had an agenda that night, and it was apparent when he picked me up, carried me to the couch, bent me over, and ate my ass. One thing Kiyan never did was eat ass! He claimed real niggas didn't do shit like that, but there he was, eating the groceries! And he did a damned good job, if I might add. By that time, my legs started to get weak from cumming multiple times, and I collapsed onto the couch.

Kiyan didn't let that deter him from his plan at all. He picked my ass up and carried me into the bedroom, threw me down on my back, and ate my vagina again. My head was so cloudy from the liquor and from the multiple times I coated Kiyan's tongue with my juices. I don't know where this energy came from, but I was ready to see what else he had in store for me. I almost jumped out of the bed when I saw him walk over to the dresser and pull out a bag from one of my favorite sex toy stores.

"Kiyan, what the fuck are you doing?" He didn't even answer me. He just walked up to me with a hard ass dick and told me to get on all fours.

I mean, I obliged the request and all, but I still wanted to know what was going on and when this nigga went to the toy store. All I know is that the good sis was NOT prepared for what happened next.

I heard Kiyan rattle a bag as he climbed in the bed behind me. Once he retrieved what he was looking for, he spread my ass cheeks apart and proceeded to lick my pussy again. This time, it was different, though. He slid a finger into my ass while licking my sweet spot simultaneously. I went through the roof! That shit felt so good, I started to buck back on his finger. Kiyan stopped abruptly though, and I whipped my head around like I had a demon inside of me.

"Why are you stopping nigg —" was all I could get out before I felt a cool, minty sensation on my vagina.

"W-what is happening, Kiyan?" He smirked and went back to eating my pussy from the back. The feeling was amazing! It was like he was using an ice cube and a cough drop at the same time.

"Get used to this type of shit, girl. I need to give your ass some act right!" he said, speaking directly to my pussy.

I came once again. Kiyan STILL wasn't done with me, and at this point, I didn't know how much more I could take. I couldn't hold my own weight anymore, and I fell onto the bed. Kiyan put my ass right back into position and told me, "naw bae, it's your fucking birthday, and you're gonna take all of this dick tonight!"

Ok, I was being punked, because who the hell was this imposter, and where was the real Kiyan? In all of the years and birthdays that I had been with Kiyan, he'd never gone this hard, and quite frankly, I couldn't figure out what to make of it.

Kiyan looked at me with pure lust in his eyes, and in his most aggressive voice, he told me, "turn your ass around." I was turned all the way the hell on now!

"Yes, Daddy!"

Kiyan went back in his little bag, and what happened next was the icing on the cake. He spread some more of whatever he had in the jar on the crack of my ass and vagina and blew his breath on me, which intensified the sensation. I later found out that the stuff Kiyan used on me is called Nipple Nibbler Tingle Balm. The flavor was peppermint mocha, and it's multi-purposed for all genital areas.

Kiyan stuck his dick inside of me, and I could've sworn that I saw stars. I couldn't catch my breath! It felt like Kiyan had grown a few inches, the way he filled me up! He was enjoying the inside of me too; I could tell by the way he moaned and yelled out my name. Kiyan started professing his love for me and telling me how good my pussy was.

I started to gain a little of my composure back and regained enough energy to fuck him back. I thought I was doing something until Kiyan picked something up and slid it across my wetness. I didn't have enough time to look and see what it was, but I certainly felt the butt plug enter me slowly.

A fucking butt plug! Whew! That thing gave a whole new meaning to nasty sex! It had to be the tempered glass one too, because it was a little cool, but not to the point of discomfort. I was in heaven between the butt plug and Kiyan's rhythmic strokes. The faster Kiyan went and the more the object went in and out of my ass, the louder I screamed and shouted to the gods about how good Kiyan's dick was. He kept pumping faster and faster, and I was now fucking him and the plug back with the same ferocity until eventually, I came again. I didn't just cum hard like the times before; I came the absolute hardest I'd ever cum in my life! Kiyan came hard too — inside of me. He didn't stop until he released every single drop inside of me. Once he got it all out, he smacked me on my ass, grabbed me by the hair so I could face him, and said, "Happy fucking birthday, bae!" We both fell out in laughter, because we both knew that we had just had the best sex of our relationship.

Kiyan and I were exhausted afterwards and fell asleep holding each other. Now why couldn't he have had this same kind of energy before? For the life of me, I couldn't understand why some people have to fuck up a good thing in order to realize the value in it. That was the last thought I had before I drifted off into a deep slumber.

CHAPTER 9

When I finally felt myself stirring about, it was around ten the next morning. I looked over to see that Kiyan was still in his pussy coma, and the thoughts about last night's fuck fest put an instant smile on my face. Kiyan never slept this late, so I knew that he must've been worn out too. I knew that he had to get up and get to the streets, so I attempted to wake him up. He wouldn't budge though, so I grabbed my phone and headed to the bathroom so that I could start my own day. I filled the tub up with my favorite Dr. Teals products and decided to soak my body because my vagina was super tender after last night's beating.

I opened my phone up once I noticed that I had multiple missed calls and text messages and began scrolling through them. Tia had texted me to let me know that she'd made it home, and so had a few other people who had attended the party.

My mom had also called, so I decided to call her back to see what she was up to. When she answered the phone, she was loud as hell.

"Hey, my newly engaged baby!"

"Hey Ma, I'm just returning your phone call. Is everything ok?"

"Yes! I'm just really excited about your engagement! I can't believe it!" she exclaimed.

"Oh goodness, Ma! Can you please lower your voice a bit because I feel a headache coming on from all the drinking I did last night."

"Girl please, you'll be alright."

She definitely didn't care about what I said and kept on with her theatrics about Kiyan being so amazing, blah, blah, blah. That was a conversation buzz kill, so I told her that I would be over there later to open up my gifts with her and quickly got off of the phone.

I believe that telling her that I would be over there later was the only thing that got her off of the phone. She actually let me hang right up.

I continued scrolling through my messages and came across a few from Torrance, reminding me about the surprise that he had for me. I had to remind myself to give him a call once I was done with my mother.

I had a bunch of birthday well wishes that I replied to before I called Tia to see what she was up to. She was another one who answered the phone loudly, so I didn't stay on long with her either.

Why was everybody so damn loud that day? Shit!

Once I was done soaking, I proceeded to get out of the tub so that I could get dressed. I was surprised to find Kiyan awake and looking through his phone. "Good morning," I said to him.

He looked up at me smiling and replied, "Good Morning."

I don't know why Kiyan was giving off the first time we met vibes, but it was pretty funny. His crazy ass jumped up and rushed me, trying to yank my towel off. I had to let his ass know quickly that there would not be any round twos today because I had stuff to do. He had finally caught the hint, walked back over to his side of the bed, and picked up his blunt to light it.

He took a few big pulls and asked, "So are you ready to be my wife?"

I truly did not want to have that discussion right then so I said, "Look, I need to get to the house with Stormy. We can finish talking later."

"Alright Joe, let me know if you need me."

I almost felt like I would need another drink to get through the day, but instead, I went to grab his blunt and puffed on it a few times.

I was not about to let thoughts of my now pending nuptials ruin a perfectly good day. I did however, finish moisturizing and getting dressed so that I could head out.

"What do you plan on doing for the day?" I asked.

"Shit, I'm about to get up and hit the streets. I have some money to pick up in a minute. Do you need some money for anything?"

"I sure do," I told him.

Now one thing I'm not, is a fool, so of course I told him that I needed some money. He pulled off a few hundreds and handed them to me with ease. I grabbed a few more out of the wad and thanked him before heading out the door.

I texted my mother when I got to my car, a Porsche Cayenne, that Fonzo had delivered to me on my nineteenth birthday.

Me: Ma, have you eaten yet?

The Queen B: no.

Me: Ok, I'll stop and get you something to eat.

The Queen B: Ok baby, thanks!

I still had to keep in mind that I'd promised Torrance that I would come over.

I wasn't really hungry, so I opted to stop and get coffee for myself at my favorite coffee place, Gloria Jean's. I ordered my mom her favorite hood meal, a fish N' chips dinner from Broadway Shrimp, and was in route to kick it with Ms. Stormy.

When I arrived, I let myself in and called out to my mother. She wasted no time hitting the staircase when she heard me. I think she only rushed down because I had some food for her. Stormy barely even spoke to me before she snatched the bag from me. "Baby, did you remember to get some extra mild sauce?"

I decided to play with her for a bit. "Dang Ma, I did forget. I'm sorry."

I saw my mother catch herself because I could've sworn that I was about to be a b-word. I didn't want to get cursed out, so I quickly told her that I was just playing. She side-eyed me before laughing.

My mom really was the most beautiful woman in the world to me. Her laugh was infectious, causing me to laugh too.

"Dang Ma, was it that serious? You were about to curse out your only child over some mild sauce."

She replied, "Pooh Butt, I love you, but I would damn near cut you over that mild sauce!"

"Sheesh Ma. Well, let me get to what I originally came here for," I said laughing.

She replied with a mouth full of food, "There isn't a rush, baby girl, just don't play about mama's food."

"I haven't eaten all morning." She announced while chewing loudly.

I rolled my eyes, and we walked into the front room, where my gifts were.

My mom began with her twenty-one questions immediately. I had an idea of what was coming, so I'd mentally prepared myself.

"So?" she started.

"Uh, so what, ma?"

"So, tell me how your first night of being engaged went. Did you put it on him Swilley style?" Stormy asked as she did a little dance in her chair.

"Ewww ma, I'm not answering that!"

That crazy ass lady told me, "Your ass better had been busting that lil' cooch wide open, considering the size of that rock Kiyan put on your finger!"

This was definitely NOT on the list of things that I was willing to discuss with Stormy today. "Ok ma, change of subject, please!"

She thought that I was hilarious or something because she started chuckling to herself. That laugh was a trap, and I wasn't falling in today.

"So, let's see what I'll open up first," I said, trying to deflect. Luckily, she got back on task and said that I should start with my dad's gifts since they were the majority. I agreed and pulled out everything that was labeled "Daddy".

CHAPTER 10

The box that I grabbed was wrapped up so pretty and had a card attached to it. The card simply read, *"To my one and only, I Love You Pooh Butt."* I couldn't resist the urge to smile at the fact that Fonzo was really trying to be better when handling me. There had been so many times that I'd wished I had a better daddy-daughter relationship with him. It never helped that everyone else around me had admired, and even idolized Fonzo. I never knew what was so special about the man who rarely smiled. Snapping myself out of my thoughts, I proceeded to tear open the pretty box.

I was super shocked to find the new season Medium Lady D-Lite Bag by Christian Dior inside. I snatched that bag out of the box fast, just to admire its beauty. I don't even know how Fonzo knew that I wanted this particular bag, but I was glad he did. My mother had the same surprised look I had. I asked her if she mentioned that I wanted this bag my father, and she shook her head no. I believed her and started with the next gift. I could only imagine what else Fonzo could have possibly gotten me. I was excited to find out. After about two hours of gift opening and constant laughs with my mother, I was finally done.

Between Fonzo and my brothers, I'd received well over fifty thousand in cash, three more designer bags, two tennis bracelets, and three diamond necklaces. I was so happy and emotional from the way my boys came through for me.

My mother and I started cleaning up the mess I'd made when I came across a few cards that I'd forgotten to open. The first one was another from Fonzo.

It read:

Dear Fallon,
There will never be another day in your life that I'll miss out on again. You are one of the most important people in my life, and I apologize for not always making you know that and feel it in your heart. Fallon, you are my one and only princess, and I am forever proud of the young woman you're growing into. No matter where I am in the world, just know that I'm always here if you need me. The material things that I purchased are in no comparison the true value that you are to me. Happy Birthday, Baby Girl! I have a few more surprises for you. First, look out the back door. After that, make your way up here to visit your old man sometime this week.
Love,
YOUR Papi

I COULDN'T EVEN CONTROL the tears that fell from my eyes as I read the card. I had been waiting for this side of Fonzo to surface for yearsssss. Better late than never! I guess it's never too late to become a daddy's girl. If he was willing to try, then so was I. Once I dried my eyes, I took off to the back door. I heard my mother trailing behind me, but I was already out the door. I couldn't believe my eyes when I saw a Challenger SRT Hellcat Redeye, customized in pink, my favorite color, sitting out back with gold rims and a yellow bow on top.

CHAPTER 11

"MA!!!!!! Do you see this?! Oh my God, I can't believe he got me this! You knew about this, didn't you, ma?"

"Well, this, yes. Nobody else that works for your dad would have gotten as detailed as me," she bragged. "The bags and other gifts I had no clue about," she told me.

I didn't even care. All I knew was that Fonzo showed his ass for my birthday. I definitely had to make some time to go see and thank him in person. In the midst of my excitement, my phone started vibrating.

When I reached for it, I saw that it was Torrance texting me.

Torr: Hey Sexy. What time are you coming over?

Shit! I had completely forgotten about my plans with Torrance, I thought to myself. I went to my mother and kissed her on the cheek.

"Ma, I'll come back over to help you finish cleaning up later. I need to make a quick run." I told her.

"Is everything ok, Fallon?"

"Yes, but I have to go," I said as I left out in a hurry. I jumped in my new car and pulled off in a rush. Once I made it to the highway, I sent a text to Torrance.

Me: Hey, I'm on my way now, I'll be there in about 20 minutes.

A few minutes later, he responded with a thumbs up emoji. I hated when niggas did that shit!

I pulled up to Torrance's condo in good timing, and I could smell food cooking before I made it to the door. I knocked softly and waited a few seconds for the door to open.

I can't front, Torrance had a really nice place. It was so nice that it didn't even look like a bachelor's pad. I joked that there must've been a woman of the house hiding somewhere.

"Naw beautiful, there is only supposed to be one woman of this house, and she is you. Are you ready to take your place in this castle?" he asked seriously.

There was definitely an awkward silence after that. After a few silent, agonizing moments, I broke the silence and said, "Whatever it is that you're cooking smells amazing."

He smiled and told me, "Real niggas cook too!" We both laughed.

"You should use that as a slogan," I said.

"Go have a seat and get comfortable. The food is almost ready."

"Ok," I shyly replied.

In the back of my mind, I knew that at some point while I was there, he was going to want some pussy.

I really dreaded it because I was in no shape to let Torrance stick that big thing he had in my still sore vagina. I was going to have to come up with something, and quick. While I was sitting at the table having small talk with Torrance, I decided to scroll on social media and see if there was any buzz about my party. To my surprise, pictures and posts about my party were trending. What got the most likes and shares was Kiyan's proposal to me. *What the fuck?!*

CHAPTER 12

The video had gone viral in a matter of hours. So many people had tagged me and asked if I had seen all of the attention me and Kiyan received. This literally was one more thing I didn't want to deal with. I sat my phone down and rubbed my forehead because I had let this thing with Kiyan get this far. Torrance saw the look on my face and asked, "Is everything alright?"

I quickly regained my composure.

"Yes, I'm fine. I'm just trying to recover from last night."

He looked at me skeptically and walked our plates to the table. The presentation of the food on the plates was amazing. Torrance really threw down for me.

He made me chicken and F-shaped waffles, stuffed French toast, cheese eggs with potatoes, and some of the crispiest pieces of bacon I'd ever had. There were Eckrich sausages and grits also. No man had ever taken the time to cook a meal for me, ever. I was so appreciative of Torrance right then. He had even gone as far as making us mimosas. I didn't even want to look at another drop of liquor, so I babysat the drink he handed me. In between sips of the mimosa, I drank the ice water that was put on the table.

Torrance and I talked, laughed and joked, even well after we'd both demolished our food. I started to see the lust dancing in Torrance's eyes as the effects of the mimosas kicked in. He drank the entire pitcher and ended up pouring himself a few glasses of D'ussé. I had to think of something before he made his move.

It was as if Torrance had been reading my mind or something because on cue, he stood up and walked to my side of the table.

"Torr, what are you doing? You're drunk; we should just cuddle for a minute," I told him.

He didn't listen to a word I said because he grabbed my hand and led me to his room. "Shit, what am I going to do now?" I whispered to myself. My brain kicked into overdrive because chile listen, I was not about to let Torrance stick that demon stick in me. My little vagina had taken enough of a beating last night, even though I couldn't tell him that. I had to switch up the narrative a little, so I turned Torrance around to face me. One thing about me is that I had mastered the art of sucking dick, so it was time for me to give Torrance the experience of his life. Once I turned Torrance towards me, I gently pushed him down on the bed. The only thing he'd been wearing was a white wife beater and some Ethika boxers. I dropped to my knees in front of him and began to pull off his shirt and boxers. My mouth watered a little as I pulled Torrance's dick out. I know it may sound crazy, but Torrance really had the prettiest penis I'd ever come across. I didn't waste any time as I went to work on his dick. I was licking and slurping on Torrance's dick like it was a slurpee from 7-11. He must've been enjoying my no gag reflex as well, because he could've been heard moaning from a block away. This nigga was really yelling my name and telling me how good the back of my throat felt.

I was getting turned on myself, but I had to snap out of it and remember the plan. Torrance really went crazy when I began rotating between his balls and dick and humming on both. I started from the shaft and let my tongue glide across the tip. I actually enjoyed giving head from time to time because I knew that I had that Throat Goat 3000.

This man started jerking and grabbing the back of my head, which only made me go harder. I mustered up as much spit as my mouth could generate and made the slurps so nasty and loud that Torrance couldn't take anymore. I happened to glance down and notice Torrance's toes throwing up gang signs as he came hard in my mouth. I'm no punk though, so I swallowed all of his babies and didn't spill a drop. Afterwards, Torrance was out like a light. I took that as my cue and got the hell out of there before he woke up. On my way out, I looked back to admire my handiwork and gave myself a pat on the back. "Got 'em!"

CHAPTER 13

When I got to my car, I hit Tia up to see what she was doing. It was normal for Tia to answer her phone on the last ring before the call got sent to voicemail, however, this time was different. She actually answered on the third ring.

"Hey Sis, what do you have going on right now?"

"Girl, not a damn thing! I'm at home bored. What are you up to?"

"Nothing major but get dressed. I'll be at your house within the hour."

"Ok, bet!"

"K, Bye," I said as I hit the end button.

Torrance lived in Calumet City, Illinois which was a good thirty minutes from Tia's house, close to mine in Merrillville, Indiana. I was in no rush though, so I took the scenic route. I wanted to show off my new car anyway. That was the reason behind me picking Tia up. We had some stunting to do. By the time I made it to Tia, she was sitting on the porch, waiting for me to pull up. The look on her face when a car she didn't recognize pulled into her driveway was priceless!

I hopped out of the car on her ass and shouted, "New car, who dis?!" She screamed and jumped up and down excitedly when she realized it was me.

"Awww shit, bitch! We about to cut up in this thang!" she shouted.

"And you know this, BITCHHHH!" I yelled back.

"Girl, I need to use your bathroom to freshen up before we go joyriding."

"Yeah girl, go ahead. You know where everything is."

She didn't care; she was recording videos of herself in my car on Snapchat.

I went in her bathroom and retrieved the hoe bag that I leave for emergencies such as this. When I was done, I put my bag up and headed back outside so that Tia and I could partake in some BHHS, or bald-headed hoe shit. We were fine as hell, and it was a beautiful day outside. This was going to be a good day! About two hours into hitting the blocks with the windows down while listening to trap music, Torrance started calling my phone. I didn't answer because I was chilling, and that's when a text message came through.

Torr: Damn, it's like that? Voicemail, huh? I just wanted to make sure you were good. You definitely didn't have to leave the way you did, but it's cool, lil' mama."

I read the message and closed the app on my phone. I wasn't replying to anything at the moment because look baby, I was on the block shooting dice with my homegirls. My phone was about to die, and I didn't have a charger. THAT was the type of time I was on!

I liked Torrance and all, but he was just way too aggressive sometimes. Plus, he wanted some pussy, and I ain't got none for him at that moment.

"Aww shit, bitch! I can see the annoyance on your face. Who did it? Was it Kiyan or Torrance? Tia asked.

I laughed and answered, "Surprisingly, it's Torrance."

She fell over in laughter. "Hell no! Not Mr. Perfect, dope dick Torrance? I can't believe that Torrance is getting on your nerves!"

"It isn't so much that he's getting on my nerves, but it's the fact that he'll blow my phone up if I don't answer or how aggressive he can get at times," I explained.

"Damn friend, really?"

"Yeah, and it's weird because I don't have those problems with Kiyan," I told her.

Tia responded with, "Bitch, you don't want Kiyan's ass anymore, so you better suck it up with Torrance. Just don't let him fuck up a perfectly good day."

I didn't quite know how to take that statement, so I just turned the music up and continued driving from block to block. The truth was that I didn't know what or who it was I wanted. I did, however, feel like maybe I should fall back from Torrance's fine ass, because sometimes that aggressive shit just didn't sit right with me.

Tia and I kicked it for a few more hours until I finally got tired of driving. We caught the attention of a few known niggas from the block, but it was nothing to write home about. It was just fun and shit talk.

Tia asked me to drop her off at her car so she could meet up with one of her sneaky links. As soon as we made it to her house, Kiyan called.

"Hey, what's up? I answered.

"Are you coming back to my spot tonight or going to your mother's house?"

"I need to come and grab a few things from your house, and then I was going back to my mom's. I planned on riding down state with her to go visit Papi."

"Aight Joe, I'll be waiting for you because I want to talk to you about something."

I rolled my eyes and simply responded with, "Ok, that's cool." Then, we both hung up.

"That sounded intense. Are you sure you'll be okay tonight?" Tia asked.

"Girl, yes! You just be safe out in these streets."

This crazy girl laughed, "Bitch, I'm always safe."

We gave one another a quick hug, and I told her to call me later. Once she was out of the car, I sat in front of her house for a few more minutes. I was honestly contemplating if I really needed what was at

Kiyan's house or just say fuck it and go straight to my mom's house. I just didn't want to have any serious discussions with Kiyan right now.

Oh, what the hell, I said to myself. I turned my music up and pulled off. *Let me see what this nigga wants.*

CHAPTER 14

When I pulled up in front of Kiyan's house, I literally just sat in my car for a minute. There was really a lot happening in my life, and I needed a second to myself.

Maybe I just need to slow down a bit, I thought, before I saw Kiyan staring at me from his bedroom window. Seeing him made me realize that he was waiting for me, so I turned the car off and got out. Once inside, I saw an open bottle of Patrón sitting on the counter. That was strange because Kiyan didn't day drink at all. My phone buzzed in my hand and when I looked down, I saw that Torrance had once again texted me. When I opened the message, I was instantly thrown off because it read:

"Who the fuck bought you a new car, Fallon?"

I couldn't believe the nerve of this nigga! I quickly responded with:

"Torrance, what the fuck is wrong with you? Not that it's any of your fucking business, but my gotdamn daddy purchased me a car for my birthday! It is not the right fucking time, so I will hit you back another time!"

I didn't even give the crazy ass nigga a chance to reply before I put him on the block list. After I took another minute or two, I proceeded up the stairs to see what was up with Kiyan and his day drinking.

When I walked in the bedroom, Kiyan was still standing in the window, with his back to me.

"Hey, what's going on with you right now?" I asked.

"Shit Fallon, you tell me." He continued, "What did you get into today?"

I was not about to set myself up, so I just cut right down to the chase. "Kiyan," I said in a composed tone. "I am not really in the mood to go back and forth right now. If you have something to say, then just say it, please."

I got hit with a jaw dropper when he asked, "Fallon, have you kicked it with any niggas in the twenty-four hours since we've been engaged?

The moment I attempted to lie, I blinked, and Kiyan was all up in my face, daring me to play with his intelligence.

"Do not fucking try me, Fallon!" he yelled.

"Get out of my face, Kiyan!" I yelled as I tried backing away from his ass, but he wasn't hearing me.

"Yo, are you really embarrassing me out in the streets? I'm out here making money, and I have people telling me that they saw you going up in some nigga's crib earlier today!"

Ok, think Fallon, you can get out of this. Just think, I thought to myself.

"Kiyan, calm the hell down and talk to me! Who the hell is feeding you these bullshit lies? I wasn't with a nigga, baby; I was with my mother earlier and then Tia after that." I saw him begin to calm down, so I kept going. "Who was fucking with your head like that, bae?"

Kiyan hesitated before telling me that he was sorry and that maybe he was indeed tripping. He walked back to the window and grabbed his drink and started mumbling something under his breath. He looked over at me and told me that he should've never let a hating ass motherfucker get in his head.

I took that as my opportunity to find out who had been trying to throw me under the bus, so I asked, "Baby, who said some stupid shit like that anyway?"

The name that came out of Kiyan's mouth might as well had been Satan's. He had the balls to let his baby mama's name fall from his lips!

I could've easily told Kiyan everything. I could've bugged up and told this man that I didn't even want to marry him and that I'd been throwing pussy to any nigga that I wanted catching it. However, when he ran up on me, I saw a side of crazy that I could only assume the niggas on the streets got to see. He would've knocked my head in between the wall and the headboard. The look was right in his eyes. I definitely wasn't in the mood to be lumped up right then, but for this nigga to stand there and be ready to fuck me up based off of what his goofy ass baby mama told him? For him to take her word as law? Nah, big fella, I'm not having that!

CHAPTER 15

I snapped! "Kiyan, you cannot even be serious right now!"

His head popped up quick. He knew he fucked up by revealing his source. "Of all the people in the world, you chose to take the word of your rat ass child's mother? A bitch who wouldn't miss a chance to have your dick in her mouth again if you allowed it?"

"Naw bae, it ain't even —"

"Shut the fuck up!" I cut him off. "You know what?" I said as I started grabbing some of my shit, "I'm gone! Go play make believe with that bitch!"

Kiyan's facial expression told me that he felt like shit when I was done with him. He didn't know if he was coming or going. It was then that he changed up, and his ass tried stopping me from leaving. I was determined to show him a lesson, though. Don't ever come at me about some he said, she said shit.

"Fal, just chill out for a second, Joe. Let's talk about this shit a little more. Stay here, bae," he pleaded.

Kiyan wanted me to stay there that night so badly, but I wasn't having it. Before I walked out of the door, I looked at him and shook my head.

"Kiyan, did you ever stop to think about the fact that she's mad because you proposed to me?"

"Did it ever once cross your mind that she wants my position in your life and would do anything to get it, including lie?"

Kiyan stood there, dumbfounded, and shook his head no.

"Of course, you didn't!" I said as I walked out and slammed the door. When I got to my car, I had the grin of the Cheshire cat on my face. I literally had gotten myself out of a sticky situation — for now.

By the time I got home to my mother's house, I was mentally tired.

All of the sneaking I had been doing was catching up to me and making me tired. I needed some good sleep, and I was at the right place for it.

When I walked in, my mother was in the kitchen throwing down. She was making fried catfish, baked macaroni and cheese with some candied yams, collard greens, and cornbread. She must've known that I was hungry, and the meal I was smelling from the driveway was right on time. I walked in the kitchen and spoke to my mom, but my eyes were on the many pots and pans in front of me.

I also noticed the Bath and Body Works candles lit as well as Summer Walker playing in the background.

"Aht Aht, this isn't for your hungry ass!"

"Ma, who else is it for then? You can't eat it all."

"Actually, it's for your father," she said.

"Um, my father who? The last time I checked, my father was in prison — not for a little while either."

Stormy looked at me and said, "See, you haven't gone with me in a while, but your dad has a few inside connections. Papi gets what Papi wants, baby." I looked at my mom like she was crazy. *Damn*, was my only thought.

My mother took out two plates and packed them with food for us to eat, while wrapping up the remainder of it for our trip the next day.

My mother and I had a really pleasant dinner that night. We laughed, cracked some jokes, drank a little wine, and spent some real one-on-one time together. I don't think she'll ever know just how badly I needed it.

I wanted to ask for her advice about my current drama, but I also really didn't want to mess up the vibe. Once we cleaned up the kitchen and put the food away, we both turned in for the night.

CHAPTER 16

When Stormy came knocking on the door the next morning to wake me up, I thought I would burst into tears. I had the most peaceful sleep that I'd had the luxury of having in a long time. There was even a little dried-up drool in the corner of my mouth. I couldn't front though; I was actually a little excited to go visit Papi. He'd hinted at possibly having another surprise for me, and I was ready to see what it was.

When I walked out of the room, I heard Jodeci's "Come & Talk to Me" bumping through the surround sound system.

"Ma!" Why are you bumping Jodeci at eight in the morning like you're on your way to see a man about a dog?!"

"Girl, shut your ass up and get dressed! Stop minding my business and mind your own!"

I didn't know what'd gotten into this lady lately, but she was giving off high school love vibes, and I wasn't sure that I liked it. I wondered if my mother had a little boo.

I made my way to the bathroom to start my morning routine. I kept thinking to myself about how peaceful and relaxed I felt after the night I had with my mom. I definitely made a mental note to make it a habit of setting aside time away from everything.

In the car, my mother continued on with her old school R&B. I was feeling it too, so I didn't complain. There was just something about old school music that fed your soul, unlike today's music. Don't get me wrong, I loved a good turn up — I was only twenty years old — however, I appreciated some good, old fashioned baby making music.

I enjoyed the long drive down state, which was about three hours long. My mother and I didn't speak a word, just vibed out to the music. When we finally pulled up to the prison, I hadn't even realized that I dozed off until the car stopped, and my mother announced that we'd made it.

I was a bit disappointed because that unexpected sleep was the best.

I looked down and noticed several missed calls from Kiyan and another unknown number. I turned my phone off.

Stormy's hot ass hopped out of the car first, straightening up her clothes and combing her sew-in out with her fingers. At this point, you couldn't pay me to believe that she burned the highway and her mileage up to simply "check" on my father's well-being. *Yeah right.*

I got out next and stretched my arms and legs out from being in one position for so long. Then, we took the food out of the trunk and headed to the prison door.

When we got to the guard station, I noticed that they barely even touched us during the routine pat search. We were also able to literally walk right in with the plates of food we brought in.

I'm no genius, and I knew that I didn't frequent this place often, but I'd seen enough movies to know that something wasn't right. That wasn't how it was supposed to go. I kept it cool though and minded my own business. Whatever Papi had going on was working well in his favor.

My mother and I hadn't waited a good five minutes before my daddy came strolling into the visiting area like he was a fucking king. He and my mom locked eyes immediately and smiled. *Aww, hell no!* They were all googly eyed and what not.

Disgusting.

Once they had broken their little secret lovers stare, Fonzo looked at me with a big smile.

"Hey, my baby girl," he sang.

"Hey Papi," I sang back.

"What's been up with you, baby? Did you enjoy your birthday?"

"Did I? Papi, it was very special. You and The Boys showed out big time!"

"Anything for you, Princess," he told me. I smiled. Big.

This exchange between Fonzo and me was everything that I had ever hoped for.

"So, are you ready for the next surprise?" he asked.

"Hell yeah! I mean, yes, Papi."

"Well, I was going to try and wait a little while longer, but this beauty queen over here convinced me to spill it."

Oh Lord, my mother was blushing.

"First thing's first, my lawyer has been working on an appeal to get me and your brothers out of prison ever since sentencing."

"Okay, and?" I pressed.

"He found something, and they granted us an appeal. We won it, so we'll all be coming home sooner rather than later!"

"Oh, my God!"

"That's great, Papi! I'm so excited!"

"Yeah baby girl, but that's not it."

"Uh ok, what else is there?"

"I'm going to finally make your mother Mrs. Jax," he said so smoothly.

At the very same time he said that, my mother held up her hand, and there was a big ass rock on her finger. Until now, I had never really paid attention to it on her finger. But now that I finally saw it, "What the fuck is happening here?!" I blurted. "Oh shit, I mean, sorry y'all, this just took me by surprise! I really am happy, guys, but how the heck have you two been keeping all of these secrets?"

Stormy was up next with answers.

"Well baby, it was kind of easy because you don't come visit often. The hardest part was not spilling the tea during one of our mommy-daughter moments. It was my decision to surprise you with that detail."

"So, is this the reason for all of the food?" I asked.

"Hell yeah," Papi said while rubbing his hands together. "Now run me my plate, daughter."

We all laughed, and my mother went to the microwave to warm the plates up for us to eat. While Stormy was at the microwave, I took that time to ask my dad about what he had going on in prison. I really wanted to know why this experience wasn't like the movies. How were we even able to get in with food and a half-assed pat down. I kind of already knew, but Fonzo confirmed it by telling me that "money talks everyday of week, baby. These guards do what I say, and I compensate them heavily."

Period.

This was the best visit that we'd ever had! I really relished in the fact that I was getting a real father-daughter experience. It was going so smoothly until Fonzo looked down at my hand and asked, "Do you have any news for me, baby girl?"

Fuck. I cleared my throat and said, "uh, yeah, Papi. Kiyan asked me to marry him on my birthday."

Fonzo had a blank stare on his face, and I couldn't read him. "Is that what YOU want Fallon?" he asked.

I hesitated before responding, "Yes."

Papi looked at me for a minute then said, "Ok."

Wait, what? "That's it? Just ok, Papi?"

"Yes, Pooh Butt. We'll revisit this conversation once I'm home, one on one."

All I could do was nod my head ok. I think Papi knew that I didn't want to marry Kiyan.

Our time with Papi lasted longer than usual this time. I was grateful for it though, because we were actually having a really good time. It started getting late, however, so Papi insisted we hit the road. I was kind of sad to be leaving. My father must've noticed the somber look on my face and pulled me in for a hug. He looked down at me and said, "Soon, you won't be able to get rid of me, Princess." I smiled and said, "I can only imagine."

Fonzo and Stormy took a few minutes to themselves. I'm pretty sure that there were fondling and doing other disgusting things in that corner, so I walked towards the front entrance and retrieved my phone. Once I powered my phone back on, more missed calls from Kiyan and the same mystery number from earlier were coming through. I was almost positive that the unknown number wasn't anyone other than Torrance, but I still wasn't answering or calling either of them back. I sent all calls to voicemail. They were on MY time now.

My mother eventually walked out with a little pep in her step. "Ugh Ma, can you stop looking like that?"

She laughed and said, "Looking like what, Fallon?"

I laughed too. "I don't know. You just look weird."

"Girl, I am happy. Get you some, boo!"

"Bye ma, you're so lame."

"Whatever. You're driving home, though," she said as she tossed me the keys.

CHAPTER 17

During the drive home, I had so many thoughts in my head. I really wanted to figure out my life and what exactly it was that I was doing with it. Upon graduation, I convinced Stormy that I would take a little time off from school and then attend college. That was two years ago, and I hadn't even thought about a college or anything associated with it. I told myself for so long that I didn't want to be a part of any drug dealing or hood love lifestyles long-term, and yet, there I was. I also wanted to know a little bit about my father's past. I wanted to know details about his upbringing. Stormy told me bits and pieces throughout the years, but I was ready for the full story.

I looked over to my mother, who was leaned back in her seat relaxing and asked, "Ma, can you tell me Papi's story?" She looked over at me, eyes as bright as ever, and said, "What do you want to know?"

With all seriousness I said, "Everything."

She sat up in her seat and began...

Fonzo's mother, Xiomara Jax, was only fifteen years old when she'd given birth to him. There had been quite a few people on the run in America coming to Cuba for refuge in the early 80's. Faraji Sanders had been one of them.

At only nineteen years old, Faraji was on the run from FBI agents in the States for his connection to The Black Panther Party as well as the growing crack cocaine epidemic. He and his friends were responsible for the distribution of the drug to thousands of poor souls all across the Midwest. Xiomara had been working for one of the local farmers, delivering fresh fruit and vegetables to the markets. She didn't make enough money to get by, but it allowed her to pay for her hostel stay and whatever necessities she needed.

Xiomara had run away from her family at only fourteen years old. Her father, Rafael, was abusive.

Rafael would come home from a long day of working in the sugar cane farms, drunk and in a bad mood. Xiomara's mother, Margarita, and her younger sister, Zenaida, would try hard to keep quiet whenever Rafael would walk in the door. Xiomara, on the other hand, was the rebellious one. She would go on as if Rafael wasn't even in the room.

Xiomara never became disrespectful or rude, however, she didn't feel the need to hide from her father. Margarita would always tell Xiomara to be quiet and keep her distance. Margarita knew firsthand how bad Rafael's temper could become, and she didn't want either of her girls to experience that. In Xiomara's fourteen-year-old mind, it didn't matter how quiet they got or how nice they were, Rafael was going to be mean and angry anyway.

One night, Rafael came home from the fields a little later than usual because he stopped at the local pub. He was hot, hungry, and frustrated. Margarita walked into the kitchen to retrieve his dinner, when Rafael, with no good reason, hauled off and slapped Margarita. Margarita was never one to back talk her husband in fear of him doing something worse, so she resumed fixing his plate.

Xiomara and Zenaida heard the commotion from their sleeping spaces and came out to see what was wrong.

"Get your ugly faces back in your room!" he slurred. Zenaida took off running, but Xiomara stayed put. He walked in her face and yelled again, "You didn't hear my command, girl?!"

"Yes father, I heard you."

"Why are you always so angry with us? What have we done to you?" Xiomara asked.

Without notice, Rafael spit in Xiomara's face and slapped her to the floor. Margarita screamed, "No!" and quickly ran to Xiomara's side.

Xiomara felt her eye close instantly.

Once she finally stood to her feet and realized what was happening, her adrenaline started to rush. She became even more enraged when she witnessed her father beating on her mother mercilessly for running to her side.

Margarita was screaming out for help, and her face was barely recognizable. Xiomara had to think fast before Rafael killed her mother. Zenaida was in the corner, bawled up and crying, which left Xiomara on her own to figure something out. Xiomara looked over and saw one of her father's empty rum bottles nearby. Moving fast, Xiomara ran to the bottle, then back to her parents. She raised the thick bottle over her head and smashed it down against Rafael's skull. When he fell over unconscious, Margarita jumped to her feet, in shock by what had transpired. "What have you done, Xiomara?" she cried.

"I was saving you, Mother! He was going to murder you!" I cried.

"Mother, is father dead?" asked an afraid Zenaida.

"I don't know, honey," Margarita replied. They all heard sirens in the distance, and that's when Margarita came to her senses.

"Xiomara, you have to go!"

A terrified Xiomara replied, "Go? Where will I go? I don't have money!"

"Yes, my daughter, you have to leave, or the government will take you! I cannot live with myself if I let them take you away, so just run, my love," Margarita explained.

"Mother, I do not want Xiomara to leave here!" cried Zenaida.

"Me either my darling, but it is best."

"I am scared, Mother. I do not know the world," cried Xiomara.

Margarita ran to her husband's side, went through his pants, and pulled out some money. She handed it to Xiomara and asked her to send notes often and let her know that she was okay once she found a place to settle into.

Xiomara agreed, gave her mother and sister hugs and kisses, then went out into the world. She learned later on that her father had indeed died from his injuries, but she knew that the authorities would still want to bring her in, so she stayed on her own. Xiomara traveled alone for what felt like days into

Little Havana, where she found work and was able to afford to rent out a room at a small hostel. It was on her route to the market of one of the farms where she met Faraji Sanders. Xiomara was headed inside the tent to the market as Faraji and a group of his friends were walking out. Faraji saw Xiomara and knew that he wanted her for himself. He whistled in admiration when he saw the young beauty, which made her blush.

Faraji and Xiomara small talked for a bit before he asked her if he could walk her home. Xiomara had no experience with the opposite sex, so she hesitated for a while before finally giving in to the young, handsome boy. Faraji told his friends that he'd catch them later. The group was fine with that because they'd managed to get into a new country with so many different fine, young women. They didn't care about what Faraji was getting into as long as he checked back in with them, letting them know he hadn't gotten caught.

Xiomara and Faraji made it to her small room, and he asked if he could come inside. Hesitantly, Xiomara agreed. Once inside, Faraji pulled a small container of alcohol out of his pants pocket, taking a swig. He asked Xiomara if she'd wanted any. Not wanting to feel excluded, she drank from the bottle. Xiomara had never been intoxicated in her short life. The liquid burned for a second and then became smooth going down. The two started warming up to one another and feeling the effects of the liquor. That night, Xiomara lost her virginity to Faraji.

The two continued on with their love affair for two more months until Faraji informed Xiomara that he and his friends needed to get back across the water and go home. Xiomara was saddened by the news, but she had to accept that Faraji was leaving. For Faraji, it was just fun. For Xiomara, it had become so much more than that.

Xiomara eventually noticed that she hadn't come on her monthly cycle the entire time that she'd been dealing with Faraji. She was no fool; she knew what it'd meant. Xiomara was devastated because she knew that she could not afford to bring a baby into the world, but she also knew that she had so much love to give the little one growing inside of her.

It was then that Xiomara came up with a plan. She would work extra hard, go into the other towns for work, and sneak into the ports in attempt to make it to America.

Xiomara worked hard all the way up until she was too tired to make those long trips. She never received any care from the local nurses, but she felt in her spirit that as long as she took care of herself, the baby growing inside of her would be fine. It was finally time to go to the local loading docks with the other immigrants who were also trying to flee Cuba. There were men, women, and children there. Everyone had their reasons for wanting to leave. Xiomara's was trying to give her unborn child a better life than what she had.

Once everyone was settled, the boat left the docks. It was a long trip with crying babies and people becoming sick from the motion of the water. Xiomara kept a positive spirit because although she didn't have a plan once they made it to America, she knew that it had to have been better than Cuba. After about a day and a half, there was an announcement that they were near the coast of Florida. Xiomara couldn't have been happier. However, she realized something was wrong when she heard a bunch of shooting and chaos. Xiomara didn't know what to do, so she sat there, frozen. People were yelling and screaming all around her. There were kids crying out because they were scared and wanted protection from their parents. It was then that Xiomara felt the wetness between her legs. She was so scared and hadn't a clue as to what she was supposed to do. Water started filling the bottom half of the boat, and that's when Xiomara realized that she needed to do something. She got off of the floor in search of an exit and now felt the pains of labor. Xiomara climbed her way to the top tier of the boat and saw blood and dead bodies all over. All she wanted to do was get herself and her baby off of the boat before they both were among the dead. Once again, Xiomara was in a position where she had to think fast!

Xiomara looked over and saw a small rowboat that had been partially let down by someone whom she could only assume tried to use it as an escape. She did her best to get it into the water intact. Another woman saw what Xiomara was doing and rushed over, wanting to also get to safety with her baby girl in her arms. Together, they worked to get the small boat in the water secured and each took a paddle to start rowing. Xiomara's pain intensified, but she was able to see the land of a new world. Xiomara kept rowing.

The unknown lady noticed Xiomara's efforts diminish and decided to take control so that they would all make it out alive. By the time they made to

Florida, Xiomara's labor was in full swing. The contractions were getting closer and closer together. In their native tongue, the woman told Xiomara that she needed to push. The woman pulled Xiomara and her own baby out of the boat and onto the sand. She laid her baby girl down and went back to Xiomara's side.

"You have to push, child!" she said.

"I can't," cried a scared Xiomara, "It's too much!"

"You have to get this baby out of you before you kill it and yourself!" Xiomara nodded her head and agreed.

Xiomara pushed and pushed until finally, she stared into the eyes of her handsome baby boy.

It truly was the first time that Xiomara felt real love. She told the unknown woman that she was looking at Fonzo Fernando Jax.

The woman smiled and walked away to check on her own baby. When she made it back over to Xiomara, she noticed that her face was draining in color. The unknown woman quickly ran to find help, when she noticed a Jamaican couple on the beach a few yards away. The woman, who eventually was known to be Belita, screamed and asked them for help. The couple quickly came to Belita's aid to see what was wrong. Once they noticed the young girl going in and out of consciousness, they began CPR. After a few attempts, Xiomara finally came to. They wrapped the baby up in their beach towel and carried her and the baby to their car.

The couple, Ace and Femi, asked Belita if she wanted to come with them to their home, but Belita declined the offer. She told them that she and her baby would be ok. They wished her luck and took off so that they could attend to Xiomara and Baby Fonzo.

As the months passed, Ace and Femi took a liking to Xiomara and especially little Fonzo. The two new house guests were more than welcomed. Xiomara was just happy that she was able to raise her baby boy in a home and love on him the way that she saw fit. It also didn't hurt that because of the lifestyle Ace and Femi lived, they were never in a position to raise a family, so they treated Fonzo like he was the son they never had.

Xiomara eventually ended up working for Ace and Femi Ebanks. They employed her as the housekeeper so that she could still attend to Fonzo daily.

As Fonzo got older, he took interest in Ace and Femi's business. He admired everything about them — the way they dressed, talked and acted. Fonzo wanted to be just like them when he got older. Femi always tried to deter Fonzo from what they were doing, but to Fonzo, Femi only wanted to baby him like his mother did, which made him gravitate to it even more. He felt like the girls were just being soft. Ace never told him no. In fact, whenever Ace would have his business meetings, Fonzo would be right there with him. In Fonzo's young mind, Ace was his dad and Ace never told him anything different. Of course, Fonzo knew that Ace wasn't his biological father, but Fonzo was Ace's little soldier, and that's all that mattered.

Xiomara didn't necessarily approve of Fonzo's interests, but the older he got, the more he didn't listen to what Xiomara was talking about. Fonzo knew at a young age that he wanted to be rich.

By the time Fonzo hit fifteen, Ace had taught him everything he needed to know about being an arms distributor. Fonzo knew all of the routes to and from Jamaica, the workers, where every warehouse was, and most importantly, where all of the safes and stashes were. Ace trained Fonzo thoroughly in the event that something happened to him or Femi.

The biggest thing that Ace and Femi did for Fonzo was make sure that he was set up. Fonzo had passports, identification cards, and money in various locations. Xiomara always felt that it was unnecessary for a child to know and have so much — that is, until the day a group of mercenaries ambushed the Ebanks's residence. They came in like something straight out of a movie. Ace and Femi defended the household until the very end. Even Fonzo had been in the mix, taking out anyone who came his way. The Ebanks, Fonzo, and Xiomara were far too outnumbered. There had to be at least forty men in the house and on the property. Femi went down first, which prompted Ace to become full of rage. His wife of twenty years was gone. Those niggas were going to pay! He raised his guns and started firing off shot after shot, taking out quite a few men. It was of no use though, because they ended up shooting Ace in the head. He was gone and Fonzo was hurt.

Before Fonzo could even process what was happening, some men snatched up Xiomara. Fonzo aimed and fired at anyone he could — until they held a gun up to Xiomara's head and told him that if he didn't drop the guns, they'd kill her.

That proved to be a grave mistake because the mercenaries raped

Xiomara in front of Fonzo before shooting her in the face and Fonzo in the chest. Hours later, Fonzo awoke and thought he was dreaming, until he looked around and saw his mother's dead body next to him. He looked over in the other direction and when he saw Ace and Femi's dead corpses, he knew that this was indeed his reality.

Ace always made Fonzo walk around with a bulletproof vest on, no matter what. It didn't matter if they were just in the house or going to the grocery store, he never wanted Fonzo to be caught off guard. It was too bad that Ace didn't follow his own rules.

Ace. Femi. Xiomara.

In the blink of an eye, Fonzo had lost everyone he'd ever cared about. He knew that he didn't have time to grieve. All of the lessons he received from Ace needed to be put to use now. Fonzo collected all of the money and guns out of the safes, took Ace's favorite car, and drove to the next Gun Pipeline in the Midwest. At the ripe age of fifteen years old, Fonzo became not just a man, but the man.

CHAPTER 18

By the time Stormy finished the story, I was fucking done! My mouth was wide open, and I couldn't even form a sentence. I would've never guessed that my daddy went through all of those things. Fonzo literally watched his mother get raped and killed, along with the other people who raised him. "No wonder he turned into a savage," I told my mother. "That's a crazy story, ma. Did he ever find Faraji?" I asked.

"Nope, he never looked for him," she said.

Damn.

After hearing that story, I was glad that we were pulling back up to my mother's house. She asked me if I was coming in, and I told her that I needed to go handle a few things. We got out of her car, I gave her a hug, and I told her that I may come over the next day before heading to my own car. I still couldn't get over how much my father overcome. I also couldn't get over how dope my new car is.

I finally had a chance to look at my phone again, and I decided to do some reaching out on my own. First up was definitely Torrance. I needed to just end things with him once and for all because the amount of stress that I was under was growing by the day. This thing with him was never supposed to be stress or work. After I dealt with

Torrance, I was going to end things with Kiyan also. There was no point in dragging things out with him anymore. The bottom line was that I was no longer happy, and now that my father was coming home, I wanted to try and focus on getting that part of my life situated.

I called Torrance and he answered on the first ring, sounding as cool as ever.

"Hey you, what's up?"

I really couldn't get a feel of him over the phone.

"Hey, can I come over so we can talk about some things?" I asked.

"Yeah, we can chop it up. Come on over. I'm at home."

On the drive over, I turned on some Jhene Aiko and vibed out. This was going to be a long evening.

I arrived at Torrance's house in about twenty minutes and killed the engine. I took a few deep breaths and got out of the car. I didn't know why, but I was really nervous walking to his door, I kept it moving anyway.

The door was cracked open as if he'd been waiting on my arrival. When I walked in, Torrance was sitting at his bar with a drink in his hand. He looked up as I approached him and smiled.

"Hey," I said.

"Hey," was his reply.

"Ok T, I'll just cut to the chase. I think that maybe we should chalk this thing between us up as a good ride that had to end. I have so many different things going on in my life, and I need to focus on that right now." I still couldn't get a solid read of his expression. There was an awkward silence, so I turned around to leave when Torrance stood up and grabbed my arm.

"Naw bae, don't leave," he said. He continued, "I just hate feeling like you're playing me for that other nigga. I want you to myself, and I made that clear from the jump."

I had to remind his ass that this wasn't just about Kiyan.

"Do you remember questioning me about who got me a car? Do you not remember that I still have parents? Regardless of all of that, you could've come at me better than that," I said.

"I know bae, and I'm sorry," he said.

Here we go.

"I had some time to think about it, and it won't happen again, bae, on my granny."

Niggas and their grannies. I shook my head, poor granny be rolling in her grave and shit. Meanwhile, he's lying his ass off. I let Torrance continue, though.

"Fallon, I know I fucked up, and I'm sorry. I just don't like the idea of another nigga doing anything for you, blood or not."

Now I knew this nigga was crazy. "Torrance, are you referring to my father buying me gifts?"

"Hell yeah!" he said. "No nigga, daddy or not, can do anything for mine."

Conversation over.

"Ok Torrance, I have to get out of here; I have to do something for my mama," I lied.

He grabbed my waist and pulled me in, then started kissing the secret spot on my neck that got me wet. He was licking and begging, which was a hell of a combination, if I might add. I tried to fake push him off, but that shit felt way too good. He started kissing lower and lower until magically, I was laid out on his couch receiving some of the best tongue action ever. This nigga was putting his whole face in my vagina, and I loved every second of it. I literally rode his tongue all the way to my orgasm. He wasn't done there either. He slid the demon that I tried so hard to rid myself of inside of me and rocked me to bliss, spilling every seed he had inside of me.

Fuck! That was some of the most toxic shit ever, but that was my life, right?

I'd never been the kind of girl to let myself get caught off guard, but on this day, all of that shit went out the window. I didn't even realize that I had fallen asleep on Torrance's couch until I woke up to Torrance, arguing and yelling on the phone with someone.

I got off of the couch and started getting dressed, when I heard him mention my name. That instantly got my full attention, so I rushed in his bedroom and noticed that he had MY phone. I ran up to him to grab my phone when I realized that he couldn't be talking to anyone but Kiyan. That was when the words he said next floored me — literally.

"Yeah, you bitch ass nigga, you remember Jay, don't you? That's my blood, nigga! Just know, if we beefing, I'll fuck your bitch! Period! She's over here sleep right now, nigga. I dicked her down, and now she's down for the count! Checkmate, you bitch ass nigga. And I'm nowhere near done either. Get at me!"

Then, he hung up.

At this very moment, I wanted to curl up and die on that floor. *Why Me?*

CHAPTER 19

I stood up, ready to fight this dude. "Torrance, what the hell are you talking about and why would you go through my phone and call my man?!" I seethed.

"Bitch, if you don't get the fuck out of my face, talking about your man." He laughed in my face. "Your THOT ass is for any nigga with some money and good dick, with your fat ass," he continued on. "I fucked you, my cousin fucked you, shit, you would probably fuck my daddy if he gamed you right. As a matter of fact, get your hoe ass out of my house! Your purpose has been served, bitch!"

I couldn't believe what was happening to me right now! These niggas had really played me. I was a part of a plot to get to Kiyan, and I fell for it. However, my name was Fallon Jax, and this nigga wasn't just about to dog me in my face and I take it.

"Torrance, one thing about you trifling ass niggas is this, y'all always think that we women are victims of yours. No, you dumb fool, this is MY vagina, and I control the narrative of IT and my life! You are absolutely right, I fucked you and your cousin. If we're being honest though, only one of y'all had good dick anyway. I'll let you guys decide who it was. Also, as far as your daddy goes, well hell, if he'll fuck me right and trick some money off, then send his old ass my way! I'll say this over and over until I turn blue in the face, I will give MY vagina to whomever I want, when I want, and wherever I want. There isn't a soul alive that would make me feel bad about that! Good-bye, you whack ass nigga! Only a lame would call another man and brag on some pussy anyway! And bitch, your mama is the fat ass," I said as I slammed the door. All I had hoped to achieve in that moment was to walk out of Torrance's house with some of my dignity, because I was really fucked up behind this new revelation, but I wasn't going to let him see that.

Now, I had to get my mind right and face Kiyan.

Fuckkkkkkkk!!!!

CHAPTER 20

I pulled off from Torrance's house and once I got far enough, I ended up pulling over in some random parking lot to figure out my next move. I couldn't believe that I had gotten played like that! How did I let my guard down like that? The sad part was that I didn't even have time to think before Kiyan started blowing my phone up. There was no way I was answering the phone for him. I still had to figure out what to say. When the phone stopped ringing, I called Tia so that I could tell her what was going on. It seemed like my life was a part of a VH1 reality show. This shit wasn't scripted, however.

Tia answered on the first ring. She told me that she was just about to call me and asked if everything was okay. "No, nothing is okay, but what made you ask me that?" I said to her.

She said, "Bitch, me and Deno were over here chilling, and Kiyan came banging on the door. He and D talked for a minute, but from what I gathered, Kiyan just left from over here looking for you, and he looked pissed!"

Shit, Kiyan never went looking for me.

"No girl," I said, "some shit happened with Torrance today. I'm going to have to fill you in later. I need to find Kiyan right now. I'll call you back, girl."

"Ok girl, be careful. Bye!"

I put the car back in drive and headed over to Kiyan's so I could face the music.

The drive to Kiyan's went much faster than I wanted it to. Luckily, when I got there, he was still gone. He was probably still out looking for me. I still hadn't returned his calls; I was going to just let him find me here whenever he got back.

As I sat in the car waiting, my phone rang. I looked down to see who it was and noticed that it was an unknown number. Reluctantly, I answered the phone, and to my surprise, it was Papi.

"Hey dad," I said.

"Hey baby girl, what's up with you?" he said.

"Oh, nothing really. What's going on with you? Is everything alright up there?"

"I know that you and your mother just left here, but I had a feeling that you needed me. Are you good?"

"Yes daddy, it's just been a long day and I'm tired," I lied.

"Ok then baby, if you need me, just say the word."

"Ok, daddy bye!"

He said his goodbye and the phone disconnected.

Even amid all of my man troubles, this new relationship with Fonzo was one of the better parts of my life. I can't honestly say why I lied to Fonzo on the phone. I guess it was one of those things where I got myself in it, and I had to get myself out of it, or so, I hoped.

Now that Fonzo and I were off of the phone, it dawned on me that when he'd called, it wasn't a regular prison phone call. I wondered about what Papi had going on up in that place. Actually, I kind of already knew; Fonzo was the man, and that didn't stop just because he was locked up. I was becoming more and more proud to be a Jax.

Snapping out of my thoughts, I remembered that I had just been freaked and sucked on. I needed to cleanse myself before I came face to face with Kiyan. Who knew, maybe the hot water would calm my nerves some, because I was a ball of nerves.

I quickly got out of the car and made a mad dash into Kiyan's house so that I could wash off the day's transgressions. By the time I gathered what I needed, got in the shower, washed myself thoroughly, and got out to dry off; I heard the alarm from Kiyan's car chirp.

For a second, I almost had a feeling of relaxation sneak up on me before it all went out of the window. I pulled out one of Kiyan's old T-shirts and awaited the blow up that was sure to come. The door slammed and I jumped. I was really scared at this point. I know that I'd said to myself for a while that I was ready to be done with Kiyan, but the threat of our demise being forced was terrifying to me. I always figured that Kiyan and I would end when and how I wanted us to, not because of someone else's intervention.

I heard a cabinet door shut, and then after a few seconds, the sounds of Kiyan's footsteps got closer and closer. By the time he made it to the doorway, I had sweat beads dripping down my neck as if I hadn't just taken a shower. He stared at me. I stared at him. I definitely didn't want to be the first one to speak. After what felt like forever, Kiyan broke the awkward silence.

"Fallon, that nigga is already a dead man walking. I want to know if you had really just got done having sex with this nigga when he called my phone."

So, this is really happening? Okay.

"Kiyan, bae it —"

"No, Fallon, fuck that!" he yelled, "Keep it fucking real with me!"

"Baby, I'm trying —" He cut me off again.

"You're not trying to do shit but lie! Now stop fucking playing, stop calling me your damn baby, and answer the question!"

Well damn, he wasn't playing around.

"It wasn't supposed to be like that, Kiyan. I promise. I was dealing with him, but I went over there to cut him off and things just kind of happened," I told him. I didn't even notice the whiskey glass in Kiyan's hand until he put it to his lips and took a sip from it. Kiyan never really was a drinker — a smoker, yes — but not a drinker. I wondered if it was me or his lifestyle that was making him drink the way that he was. Kiyan snapped me out of my thoughts when he threw the whiskey glass at the wall, right past my head and it shattered. It took me a minute to realize what was going on. I surely wasn't used to Kiyan doing such impulsive things. Before I could ask him why he would do some shit like that, he ran up on me, fast! Kiyan was up on me with both of his hands around my neck, quicker than I could blink. He snatched me out from the spot on the bed that I had been occupying and had me pinned up in a corner of the room, against the wall. Kiyan was really putting his hands on me, and I was in disbelief.

"Let me go, Kiyan!" was all that I could manage to get out.

"You better let me the fuck go before I tell Papi!" I screeched.

"I don't give a fuck about no damn Papi; that nigga probably doing one hundred life sentences anyway!" he seethed.

Kiyan wasn't even present anymore; he was a totally different person. Whoever this person was in front of me was absolutely terrifying, and I felt like he was actually going to kill me.

I kept fighting, though.

"Kiyan, get the fuck off of me!" Still nothing, but I had noticed that Kiyan's eyes were bloodshot red. "Kiyan, you're killing me," I tried once more, but I couldn't even hear myself anymore, and I felt like I was slipping away. Kiyan was much taller than me, so there wasn't much I could do to get him off of me. I felt the room getting darker as I felt my breathing get more and more shallow. All I saw was darkness, and I wondered if I had finally pushed Kiyan over the edge.

Once upon a time, I actually loved this man unconditionally — that is, until he showed me that there were indeed conditions to love. *I can't believe we let things get this far,* were my last few thoughts before there were no more.

I guess that brings me to the here and now...

CHAPTER 21

When I finally came to, I didn't have a clue as to what time it was or even how long I had been out. All I knew was that I was laid across Kiyan's bed, and my throat felt like it was on fire. I never in a million years would've guessed that Kiyan was capable of putting his hands on me, no matter how mad he'd gotten at me. Kiyan? No.

Kiyan kept that street shit in the streets. He never showed me that other side of him — until today.

As I rose up, I rubbed my throat and noticed Kiyan sitting in a chair in the corner of the room with yet another whisky glass filled to the brim. He'd also taken the liberty of cleaning up the shattered glass that was on the floor. I didn't quite know what to expect right then, but I knew that I needed to get away from Kiyan before he made another violent move towards me.

I stood and tried to gather my things to leave when Kiyan said to me in a low growl, "Fallon, sit the fuck down. Now."

I froze.

"Kiyan, you've made your point, and now I'm leaving. I'll leave your ring, if that's what you want," I told him. Kiyan looked at me with blood-stained eyes and said, "I'm not going to say it again."

Now, I know that I could pop my shit from time to time, but Kiyan's demeanor and the fact that that he'd just choked me out made me follow his demand. So, I sat my ass back on the bed.

"Kiyan, what more do you want? You've already put your hands on me; there isn't much more that I'm going to take from you."

He jumped up and got in my face and said so disrespectfully, "You going to take whatever the fuck it is that I want you to take! The problem with you, Fallon, is that I've given you too much freedom and room to do whatever your spoiled ass wanted to do; and you've mistaken me for some weak ass nigga! News flash," he stated, "I'm not!"

"Bae, it was never my intention to hurt you, but I myself, was hurting," I confessed. That was me being honest. He looked at me as if I had said something wrong.

"Fallon, what the fuck could your selfish, spoiled ass be hurting from?!" he yelled.

"Kiyan, you can't be fucking serious right now!" Now, I was yelling. I continued with, "I've been expressing my unhappiness for months now! You chose to ignore me! The fact that you were so damn careless in doing your own bullshit that you brought a baby to my doorstep still fucks with me! The fact that I have to deal with your ratchet baby mama, who is in love with you and your money, still hurts me as if it happened yesterday! I have never been okay with any of this shit; I've just been managing! I aborted my own fucking baby because of all of this shit, so don't act like all was forgiven or forgotten just because you apologized and put an engagement ring on my finger!"

By this time, I was in my feelings, and the tears were non-stop — on top of my throat burning from being choked. I still wasn't done yet, though. I kept on with my rant because it was now or never.

"If I'm being honest, Kiyan, I haven't been happy since you told me about Kiyari being on the way. I didn't know how to express it to you, so I cheated. I cheated because it made me feel good to get back at you. I cheated because I felt as if I was hurting you the same way you hurt me. I cheated because it wasn't fair that I was able to give you my all and the best of me, but you had to be selfish and want more. I cheated because the moment you cheated on me, you broke me in ways that even the biggest ring in the jewelry store couldn't fix. Lastly, I cheated because it felt good to be wanted — no matter how temporary the feeling was — by someone who hadn't betrayed my trust. Kiyan, you would've known all of these things had you paid a little more attention to me. I've been drowning with no one to save me."

There it was. Everything that I'd been needing to say to Kiyan for the longest time. I truly hated that it had to be under these circumstances for the truth to finally come out. We were both in tears.

Was this really love?

All of this had me questioning what love really was.

CHAPTER 22

Kiyan was eerily quiet. There was, however, one more thing I needed to get off of my chest.

"Kiyan," I began, "if there is one thing that I do regret out of all of this, it would have to be me going through that entire abortion ordeal."

"Don't put that shit on me, Fallon. I didn't want you to go through with it either. You really didn't have to," he responded.

"Yeah Kiyan, I actually did. You don't know the turmoil I felt knowing that you gave someone else a gift that was supposed to be set aside as a first for us. I thought that I was doing the right thing for me, and now, I don't feel like that was the best decision. I think I would've been a damned good mother," I sighed.

More tears. We were both hurting.

Kiyan stood and walked over to me. He stood directly in front of me and kneeled down so that we were face to face. He wanted me to look him in his eyes, but I couldn't do it. If I was being honest, Kiyan being this close to me had me a little spooked after he choked my ass to sleep.

He put his hand to my face and gently wiped away the tears that were spilling down my face, which prompted me to do the same for his falling tears. It was this small gesture that made me remember the good days we used to have.

Kiyan went from swiping at my tears to gently caressing my now bruised neck. He softly placed his head in my lap, which led me to rub his head. After a minute or so, Kiyan began kissing on my inner thighs. He went from kissing on my thighs to laying me back on the bed and leaving a trail of kisses down my legs, stopping at my feet. Kiyan gently raised my feet to his mouth, and one by one, kissed and sucked on each one of my white painted toes. Even during our toughest moments, he still managed to surprise me with new things. I didn't stop him; it felt so good. Once he was done there, he stood up and pulled down his pants, hovered over me, and inserted his penis inside of me. Kiyan rocked inside of me so sweetly. He looked me deep in my eyes and never looked away. This was intimacy in its highest regard, but it was also toxicity in its even higher form.

Still, I never pulled back from it. I was fully engulfed in this lovemaking.

Kiyan's strokes had my eyes rolling to the back of my head. It was like I could feel every pulsating vein on his dick, rubbing against my walls, creating the best friction imaginable. It was kind of like he had a point that he needed to prove, which was fine with me. I had gotten so wet for Kiyan, and he was loving every moment of it. He raised my legs over his shoulder so that he could go deeper, and that was where he fucked up. The harder he pumped, the closer to an orgasm he came, until finally, he couldn't take it anymore and spilled his seeds inside of me. I came with him, really hard.

Once we were finished and he rolled off of me, it was back to the awkward silence. I had a strange feeling come over me that made me feel as if we had just fucked up. I think Kiyan felt it too. Of course, my dumb ass decided to break the silence with, "So what now?" *Really Fallon? That was the best you could come up with?*

Kiyan sat up in the bed, and just as he was about to respond, his phone started ringing. He walked over to his pants that were now on the floor, and grabbed his phone out of the pocket. I could tell by the look on his face that he didn't really want to answer the phone.

"Who is that?" I asked, fearing that it was Torrance still keeping up trouble. To my surprise, it wasn't Torrance but yet another thorn in my side — Terica.

I instantly became pissed off, and as Kiyan answered the phone, I found some clothes to throw on, and I got dressed to leave. Once Kiyan realized that I was leaving, he began rushing Terica off of the phone. She must've sensed what he was doing because I heard her ghetto ass from where I was standing, asking him why he was rushing her off the phone. That made him become irritated, and he told her to text him whatever it was she wanted for Kiyari before he hung up.

"Where the fuck do you think you're going, Fallon?" he asked.

"Home," is the only reply I offered him.

CHAPTER 23

"Home? What do you mean, home? We aren't done here, you'll leave when I want you to leave!"

I scoffed at his bravado in that moment.

"Kiyan, look, the dick was amazing just now, and the fact that we still love one another is evident. Our problem- the reason I feel the way I do- is who you just hung up on."

"There will never be peace for you or for us," I told him.

"Fallon, I know that I choked you to sleep or whatever, but did you slide into a coma and forget that a nigga, who you've been cheating on me with, called to brag about fucking you out of revenge for his cousin, a nigga you also fucked? The same nigga who burned you, which in turn made you burn me?"

"I know you aren't slow enough to believe that everything we're going through is solely on me," he continued. "I know I fucked up royally, Fallon. You just can't get a nigga back like that though, ma."

"Fuck you, Kiyan!" I yelled, now embarrassed.

"No Fallon, fuck you! I actually love your fat ass! Even with all of our issues, I was still willing to wife you so that we could get through all of our obstacles as a team, but nope, Fallon can't keep that pretty little kitty to herself!"

I was so thrown off by Kiyan's words that I had no rebuttal this time. That was it, though. These niggas had Fallon Jax fucked up today! I charged at Kiyan full speed and yelled out, "You motherfuckas aren't going to keep calling me fat today!" while swinging on him. Kiyan was caught off guard as well, but he was able to catch me mid swing and put me in a bear hug. "Fallon, stop it!" he urged.

"No nigga! Let me the fuck go!" I yelled and struggled to get free at the same time.

It was of no use. Kiyan was taller and stronger than me. I felt depleted. It was as if every single thing and feeling that I'd put to the side for the past few months had caught up to me in that moment. I just broke down right there in the arms of the person I hated and loved the most.

When Kiyan realized that my anger and rage turned into pain and tears, he let go of the firm hold he'd had on me. He hugged me with all of the love he held for me. I cried one of those ugly, snot-filled cries, and he stood there and rocked me through it all.

I probably will never forget this moment because it was a low one for me. This was, however, the moment I realized how faulty I was. I pulled back from Kiyan's hold and composed myself. I felt so transparent and broken. I didn't know what else to do at that point, so I grabbed my purse and told Kiyan that I needed to leave. This time, he didn't try to stop me, and for that, I was grateful. He did call my name and when I turned around, he said, "You said something earlier, and I want to know what it meant."

"What is it, Kiyan?" I replied.

"Is your dad coming home or something?" he asked.

"Yup," I said and walked out.

I left Kiyan's house with a heart so heavy, I didn't know what my next move was going to be. There was still so much that needed to be said and done as far as Kiyan went, but I couldn't handle anything else at this point. My life had been completely blown up in a matter of hours, and there wasn't a thing I could do about it.

. . .

I JUST NEEDED some time to myself for a little bit, and that's just what I did. I took out my phone and booked me a room at The Nobu Hotel, which is in Downtown Chicago. I plugged the address into my GPS and started my journey. I hadn't packed any clothes or toiletries since this was an impromptu mini vacation, so I figured I'd just go shopping while I was there. A little retail therapy was good for the soul anyway. There was some light traffic, so it took me almost an hour to make it to my destination, but once I arrived, I felt like it was well worth it.

I gave my keys to the valet driver and proceeded to the desk, where I checked in and got my keys. I took my time walking to the elevators because this hotel was beautiful. I appreciated the scenery because it wasn't often that I made my way to Chicago, and I'd never just booked a hotel room to get away from everything. This was different for me.

CHAPTER 24

When I opened up the door to the room, I was in complete awe! This room, well suite, was amazing! I just knew that I was going to get exactly what I was looking for here — a piece of mind. I had booked it for the week so I was good to go.

I took a mini tour around the luxury suite before I bounced back to reality. Before I settled and made myself comfortable, I had to go to find a store and pick up the few things that I needed. This hotel had a restaurant in it, so I wasn't worried about food. I googled the nearest Walmart and Target near me. Neither were that far, so I opted for the closer of the two, which happened to be Target.

I took my time perusing the store because time was on my side, and I didn't have a damn thing better to do at that moment. I walked and shopped until I was ready to go. Once I made it back to my room, I pulled out my phone to let my mother know that I had come for a little get away, and that I would see her in a few days.

I also made sure to let her know that I needed a spa day with her and that if anyone was looking for me, she was not to give my whereabouts.

Of course, Stormy's nosey behind wanted to know what was going on immediately, but I had to convince her that I was fine. I just needed some alone time. She accepted that answer and told me that if I needed her, she'd always be there. I truly knew that though.

For the next few days, it was all about me. With my mother knowing that I was okay, I powered my phone off, threw it in my purse. I ran me a nice, hot bubble bath. While the bathtub was filling up, I went into the kitchen area and poured me a glass of the wine I'd picked up from the store. A soft red wine always set the mood. Luckily, I found a nice gentleman willing to purchase alcohol for a minor. I'm sure that the one-hundred-dollar bill I compensated him with was what did the trick.

After pouring my wine, I checked to see if my water was ready. It wasn't, so I walked over onto the balcony to take in the beautiful view once more. Chicago really was an amazing city, aside from the crime and violence. Hell, right now this beautiful city was giving me exactly what I needed in the moment — peace.

By now, my bath was ready and so was I.

Once I was fully submerged, I felt all the stress and burden melt away. I sat and let the Dr. Teals products, along with the scalding hot water, do their jobs for over an hour. I got tired of refilling the water when it got cold that I reluctantly washed my body, rinsed off, and got out.

I walked over to the bed with a towel wrapped around me and plopped down. I was really enjoying this quiet time. I felt some relief. I went inside the many bags from my Target run and grabbed the baby oil gel so I could moisturize myself. It was the best that I could do since I didn't have any of my normal toiletries with me.

When I finished doing that, I turned on the TV and got comfortable in the bed. I flipped through the channels until I landed on an episode of *Snowfall* and decided to watch it. I loved me some Franklin Saint! It wasn't long before I had fallen asleep.

When I had finally awakened, the sun was out and the TV was playing reruns of the show *Atlanta.* I looked over at the clock that read eleven o'clock am. I couldn't even recall what time it was that I went to sleep, and I didn't even care.

I was hungry, so I decided to see what the hotel's restaurant had to offer downstairs. I went in the bathroom and took care of my hygiene, got in the shower, and put on one of the outfits I found in Target. It wasn't what I was used to, but I made it work.

Once I took a look in the mirror and did a glance over my appearance, I decided that I was good and grabbed my purse to proceed downstairs.

I made it to the restaurant in time for the start of lunch, which was fine by me. The waitress took my order and as I waited for my food to arrive, I noticed a nice piece of chocolate staring at me. He smiled and so did I. I'm assuming that he took that as a signal to approach me, because that's exactly what he did.

Mr. Tall Dark and Handsome stepped to me, smelling so good and looking so fine. He introduced himself as Legend. I smiled and introduced myself as well. When Mr. Legend asked if he could join me, I politely told him no. He couldn't believe it. My guess was that no one had ever used the word no when dealing with him.

Legend took the sting of my rejection and walked off. That was fine with me. The truth was, I was taking this time for myself. I needed to figure Fallon out at this moment. I had more than my fair share of man drama going on right now. I could've given Mr. Tall, Dark and Handsome an explanation, but I didn't owe anyone shit. No is no — period. If it had been another time and under a different circumstance, he may have had a chance.

CHAPTER 25

My food arrived shortly after Legend left. It tasted just as good as it looked. I ordered the lamb chops with garlic mashed potatoes and roasted asparagus. The shit damn near melted on my tongue. When the waitress came back and asked how everything was, I asked her for the name of the chef because he'd done a phenomenal job.

She told me that his name was Chef Ty, and I told her that I wanted to leave a tip for not only her, but for the chef as well. She thanked me for the compliment, I paid my bill, and returned to my room. On my way to the elevator, I saw Legend staring at me with lust written all over his face.

I did what every female does when she knows that a man is watching. I put a little extra wiggle in my jiggle as I boarded the elevator. I saw him smile and wink at me as the doors closed. Just because I was soul searching didn't mean that I couldn't flirt a little.

When I reached my new sanctuary, it put a smile on my face to realize that I had no obligations- no running errands or no sneaking off to meet anyone. It's such a shame that at twenty years old, I was having to run away from the world and the chaos I'd created just for a little peace. I wasn't willing to give it up ever again. My peace had to be protected at all costs moving forward.

I took in the opportunity to get some more well needed rest and decided to take a nap. I loved naps; I think that's the part of adulthood I like best.

It was two hours later when I opened my eyes. I stretched, got up, and decided that I was hungry again. This time, I ordered from DoorDash. I sat in my room and ate, watched TV, took long, hot bubble baths, and repeated that for the entire week I was in that hotel, never turning my phone on once.

During my time of solitude, I did come to the conclusion that I wanted to go back to school. I didn't believe that I would run into any issues, considering the better than good grades I received in high school.

I always told myself that if and when I decided to enroll back in school, I would take up real estate. I'd always loved the inner workings of investing into property and flipping it for profit. I also liked watching those home improvement shows on TV, and I had a knack for interior decorating as well.

Whatever it was that I would do, I just knew that I had finally come up with a plan for my life. I couldn't have been happier with myself.

It was time to check out, and I was so sad to be leaving. I promised myself that I would do things like this more often, just to reset from whatever life threw at me. I didn't bother taking any of the things I had purchased with me because I probably would never use any of it again.

When I took my purse and headed down to turn in my keys, I bumped into Mr. Chocolate, aka Legend. We locked eyes, and while I was handing the lady at the front desk my key, he approached me, once again smelling good and looking fine. I asked the cutie if there was something I could help him with, and he responded, "Hell yeah, but you playing, shawty."

"Is that an accent I hear, Mr. Legend?" I asked.

"Yeah shawty, I'm from Memphis," he said in that sexy southern accent.

Now how did I miss this before? Lord, be a fence and a shield! "Memphis?" I asked.

"Yeah, Miss Lady, why? You got peoples down there?"

I hit his ass with, "Yup, my Uncle Clifford and cousin, Mercedes, live over in Chucalissa and work down there at Pussy Valley."

I'm dumb, I know I thought to myself for giving him names and locations off of the popular TV show P-Valley on the Starz network.

"Naw, I don't know them, boo, but I wanna get to know you," was his answer.

"I'm good, love. You have a good rest of your day, though," I said as I walked to the valet and retrieved my car.

When I finally sat in the driver's seat of my car, it felt weird, like it was the first time. I shook the feeling, powered my phone back on, and found some music to vibe to on my way home. The first song that bumped through my speakers was *Imported* by Jessie Reyez and 6lack. I loved the song, so I turned it up, but not before I heard numerous notifications coming through. I ignored them all and proceeded home. I actually missed Miss Stormy, soon to be Mrs. Jax. How weird was that? I laughed to myself and pushed through the traffic.

Finally, I pulled up to my mother's house, and I didn't feel like parking in the garage, so I left my car in the driveway and went inside. The smells coming from the kitchen and the sounds of Stephanie Mills's *I Feel Good All Over* led me right to my mother. Stormy was throwing down on some oxtails and rice, which was one of my granny's recipes that my mom had mastered.

In the week that I was at the hotel, I sure did miss my mother's home cooked meals, so the smells from the pots on the stove made me weak with hunger. However, I didn't overlook the fact that my mom seemed to be glowing, and she only listened to this particular song when Papi was involved. I told myself that I would be nosey later on because at the present moment, I was about to dig into this food. "Hey ma," I said.

"Well, hey yourself, stranger. How are you feeling, baby?" she smiled.

"I am really good, mommy and also really hungry, so let's talk while I make this plate," I said while rubbing my hands together in anticipation for some good ol' food.

"Go ahead, baby, help yourself," she said.

"Dang ma, why did you cook so much? Did you know I was coming?" I laughed.

"Because she feeds your daddy well," said Fonzo.

CHAPTER 26

"Oh my God, Daddy you're really here!" I was so excited that I dropped the utensils on the floor and ran into Fonzo's arms.

Fonzo laughed a hearty laugh, "Yeah, Pooh Butt, I told you I was coming!"

"I'm saying though, daddy, you didn't have to tell on nobody or nothing like that, did you?" I just really needed to know.

"GIRL, hell no! I live by a certain code, ain't none of that going on around here! I already told you that my attorney is one of the best to do this shit and won mine and your brothers' appeals. They'll all be out here in a few weeks. Somehow, none of the witnesses turned back up," he explained.

Oh Lord, I know what that meant, so I just replied with, "Oh, ok." I'm going to leave that topic alone and just enjoy one of the first meals I got to share with my parents together.

"So, tell me about your week," Fonzo said.

"Well, um, it wasn't really that interesting, Papi. I just needed some time to myself, that's all."

I probably would've felt a little better had I just trusted my parents with what was happening in my life, but I was more embarrassed than anything.

"Why don't you sound sure about that, Fallon?" asked my own personal lie detector, Stormy.

"Ma, I'm fine. How long have you been home, daddy?" I deflected.

"I've been here for as long as you've been gone. I called your phone and got sent to voicemail, and that's when your mother informed me of your "vacation".

"Oh, yeah, I just needed some me time," I told him.

At last, the direction of the conversation had changed from about me to what was going on in the news and in the neighborhoods. I was grateful for that. We were all nice and full, at least I know I was, and decided to go our separate ways. My mother and father went to their room, which was definitely going to take some getting used to. I headed to my own bedroom. Once I got comfortable in my bed, I took out my phone to finally see what my hundreds of notifications were about.

I had to put my air pods in my ears because I could hear the sounds of R. Kelly playing from down the hall, and that just didn't sit well with me. The first few texts that I read were from Tia, asking me what was going on and if I was ok. I decided that I would reach out to her first thing tomorrow. I also saw that I had text messages from Kiyan asking if we could talk, which prompted me to roll my eyes. There was nothing for us to discuss. I did remember the ring that was still on my finger and made a mental note to have it returned to his ass ASAP.

The bruises on my neck had gone away, but not the memories behind it.

I had multiple notifications from all of my social media accounts. I didn't check them all, but I did see a few posts that I knew were about me on one of Torrance's pages. He basically tried to clown me, speaking on a certain "hoe" he'd fucked and his cousin as well. I wanted to really beat his ass, but I was taking the high road, so I just blocked his goofy ass.

On second thought, maybe I just needed to put the phone away and continue on with my peaceful day. This time, I put the phone on Do Not Disturb and decided that I would catch up on my ratchet TV shows that I loved so much on VH1 and a few that were on BET.

After what must've been a few hours later, I heard a light tapping on my door.

"It's open," I said.

In walked Papi with his hair freshly braided in his signature style. My mother did a good job.

"Hey Papi, what's up?" I asked.

He said, "I could ask you that same question." I was puzzled.

"What do you mean?" I asked him.

"Tell me what nigga put his hands on you," Fonzo demanded.

I stammered. "I uhhh —"

"Fallon, don't lie to me." He cut me off.

"It was Kiyan, but Papi, it wasn't like that, and you have no idea what led to it!" I cried.

Papi was way too calm and I was nervous. I was more scared for Kiyan, though, so I felt the need to protect him from the monster known as Fonzo Fernando Jax.

"Papi, please say something," I urged.

"There isn't anything to say, Pooh Butt. Goodnight."

That couldn't have been it. I had to do or say something. "Dad, wait! Let me at least tell you what's going on. Please."

"What is it, Fallon?" he asked.

I wasn't sure if it'd mean anything or not, but I told Papi everything, even the parts I was most embarrassed about. By the time I was done, my eyes were puffy and I felt silly, but it felt good to let it all out.

CHAPTER 27

I couldn't get a clear read of Papi's face, however, and that made me paranoid. I needed to know what he was thinking and what his next moves were. He never interrupted me, not even once. I was able to get everything out, and he just sat there taking it all in.

"Dad, say something, please," I begged. He looked over at me and pulled me in for a hug. "I see where I went wrong with you, and I am sorry. There is no fucking way that any daughter of mine should be out here playing herself for these nothing ass niggas. You are Fallon fucking Jax and you are street royalty! A fucking queen! These niggas thought that because I was in that cage that shit was sweet, and again, that's my fault, but I'm here to fix this shit now!"

"Does my mom know about the bruises on my neck?" I asked.

"No, I wanted to get the truth from you, and I didn't want to worry her with that. She needs to be focused on being as fine as she is and planning her perfect wedding. I'll deal with the rest," he said.

I had another question because I hadn't been around anyone who could've possibly seen my neck, so I asked, "How did you know about my neck anyway?"

Fonzo chuckled and replied, "Girl, I'm your damn daddy. The

minute Stormy told me that you were going to some damn room for whatever reason you gave her, I sent one of my young boys up there to keep an eye on things."

Young boy? I thought to myself. Who the hell could he be talking about? Then it dawned on me. "The dude, Legend?" I asked in disbelief.

"Yep," was all Papi said before he kissed me on the forehead and walked out.

I cannot believe that Legend worked for my damn father! I thought he was just persistent, I laughed to myself. It felt so damn good to be able to tell my problems to my father, the one who's supposed to be my protector anyway. Even though Kiyan and I were on bad terms, I never would want to see him hurt. I didn't know what Fonzo's plans were, but I'd hoped that after everything I told him today, he'd leave Kiyan out of it.

After the draining conversation I just had, I felt the need to call it a night. I turned the TV off, turned my fan on, and was knocked out. And yes, I am one of those people who can't sleep without a fan, no matter if it was eight degrees or eighty degrees outside.

It was around four in the morning when I woke up from a deep sleep and ran to the bathroom to expel all of the contents in my stomach. It was mostly the eggs that I'd eaten at the hotel, so I didn't think anything strange was going on, outside of a bad hotel breakfast. I brushed my teeth, rinsed with mouthwash, and went back to sleep. I woke up again around eight-thirty and felt really confident about what the day would bring. It was Monday morning, and I was ready to set my plan into motion. Today was the day that I was going to enroll in one of the best local real estate programs around. Maybe that was the reason behind me hugging the toilet a little while ago. Nerves. This was a big deal for me, and I couldn't wait to tell my parents the news.

I got out of bed, brushed my teeth, and showered. When I was fully dressed, I headed downstairs to see what Stormy and Fonzo were up to. My mother was in the kitchen, looking as beautiful and radiant as ever, while doing her magic in the kitchen, whipping up some breakfast.

"Good morning, beautiful," I sang.

"Whew! My baby got that 20/20 vision, telling me what I already know! No seriously, good morning, my beautiful daughter," she joked.

"It smells good down here, ma. Where's Papi?" I asked her.

"Oh, he cut out after he ate. He had some business to take care of. This right here, that I'm making, is for you," she informed me.

"Aww, thanks mommy. I'm not going to eat much, though. I have a few things to take care of as well today," I told her.

"Okay baby, that's fine. I'll just see you later then. I have a wedding to plan anyway." She did a little dance while saying that.

I rolled my eyes and told her not to do too much, and this crazy ass lady had the nerve to tell me, "I am too much, daughter!"

And on that note, "Bye ma!" I yelled on my way out of the door.

It was such a beautiful day outside. I took in the fresh air and decided that I needed to get my car washed. She was too pretty to have dust on her. I got in and opted to listen to some MoneyBagg Yo. I felt like a little trap music would do me some good.

My first stop of the day was to McColly School of Real Estate. I didn't have to make an appointment, so I wanted to be there as soon as they opened. When I got there, the owner and instructor, Kim, was there. She was very friendly, and it just so happened that the company I chose to go through was a black-owned company.

Mrs. Kim took great care of me while I was there. When we were done, I'd made my payment in full and decided to take the twelve-week course, which was due to begin in one month, which would be August first.

I felt like I was floating on a cloud. Just the thought of me doing some positive for my future had me ecstatic. I wanted to share my good news, so I called Tia.

CHAPTER 28

I felt bad because I hadn't really been in touch with Tia, and I knew that she was genuinely concerned about me, but I needed to get me together first. I'm sure that she would understand. I almost regretted calling, however, because as soon as she picked up the phone, there was a cloud that started hovering in the sky.

"Hey bitchhhh!" I greeted.

"Naw, don't hey bitch me, are you ok, Fallon? I've been worried sick, and nobody knew where you were. What's going on?" she asked.

"Girl, there was just so much happening at one time. I just needed some time to myself. I have some good news, though," I stated.

She replied, "girl, me too, but you go first."

I was more than happy to go first, so I yelled into the phone, "I enrolled in McColly Real Estate School todayyyyy!" She seemed to be happy for me because she screamed right along with me. That made me feel a little better. I was glad that we able to fall right back into our routine without it being weird. I was ready for her news now, so I urged her to spit it out.

"Bitch, I am pregnant, and me and Deno decided to move to Atlanta!"

"Oh, my God! I'm so happy for you, friend! How far along are you? I can't wait to be an auntie!" I shouted.

"Girl, we found out the night Kiyan came banging on the door looking for you. I didn't know what was going on, so I was trying to wait until we really talked before I told you.

"That's some really good news, T. You should've led the conversation with that," I laughed. I knew that she and Deno had been messing around for a while now. He was one of Kiyan's friends.

She stopped laughing and got serious when she said, "That's not all that I need to tell you, though."

Just like that, the cloud opened up and it started to rain. "What is it?" I begrudgingly asked.

"Early this morning, Torrance was found hanging from his bedroom window. I heard that he was badly beaten and his tongue was cut out of his mouth," she informed me.

"Are you serious?" I asked in disbelief.

"Girl yes, I couldn't believe it either when I heard it."

"That's crazy," I said.

"I know, right. Are you going to be okay?" she asked.

"Yeah girl, I'm just shocked by that news, that's all," I said.

"I'm just checking. I know that you two were pretty close."

"Yeah, we were. Okay, best friend, I have some more errands to run; I'll call you when I make it home," I told her.

"Okay girl, I'll talk to you later, bye."

I found myself not able to breathe, so I just hung the phone up. I didn't know what to think or do right now. Somebody did Torrance really bad, and I didn't know if it was Kiyan or my damn daddy.

The rain started to fall harder at that point, so I took my ass home. I needed to see Fonzo and find out if he knew anything about what had happened to Torrance. Just based off of Torrance's hidden agenda with me and the terrible things he'd said to me alone, made me not truly care about his outcome. The only concern I had was whether or not my father or ex-fiancé were involved. I had just gotten Fonzo back, and I wasn't willing to lose him because I made a mess that he cleaned up. I didn't want to see anything bad happen to Kiyan either.

By the time I returned home, both my mother and father were there. They had been chilling in the front room watching a movie. I was completely surprised to see Legend, sitting with them as well. Now that I thought about it, there was an unfamiliar car in the driveway that I hadn't paid any mind to.

"Well, hey y'all. What's up?" I said coolly.

"Hey baby," both my parents said in unison.

"You look bothered, Pooh Butt. You good?" Papi asked.

"I'm good," I said, "but I didn't know we were having guests."

"What's good, shawty? Why I gotta be a guest? I can't be extended family?" Legend said amused.

"Ha, ha, ha. Very cute," I said in response.

"Ma," I whined.

"Unt uh, Fal, I'm watching my movie. Don't kill my vibe," Stormy said.

They all started laughing at my expense, so I rolled my eyes at Legend and went to my room.

CHAPTER 29

When I got inside of my room, I plopped down on my bed. Why was Legend so damn fine?! I am in recovery mode from the hoe life, and Papi wanted to bring this fine ass piece of chocolate around me and kick me off of the wagon. This cannot be my life right now. Just as I was about to change into some lounge wear to relax, I heard a knock at the door.

"Come in," I said. Once again, Fonzo walked in and sat on the bed next to me.

"What's up, Pooh Butt?" he said.

"Nothing much, daddy. Just about to chill for the evening. What's up with you? I see you were out early today," I hinted.

"Yeah, the early bird catches the worm. You know that. I had some shit to handle," Fonzo said confidently.

"Shit like what, Papi?" I wanted to know. Before Fonzo could reply, my phone started going off, and it was Kiyan. As I was about to send him to voicemail, Papi stood up and said, "You might wanna answer that. You two have some shit to talk about."

"No, we don't. I'm going to return his ring to him and that's going to be all," I said cockily.

"Ok, you can do that, but you also need to tell him that you're pregnant," Fonzo said.

"Papi, what are you talking about? I am not pregnant!" I told my father with conviction.

He really laughed at me and said, "Pooh Butt, trust me. I've gotten enough women in my life pregnant to know. Y'all figure that out on your own, though. Let me get back out here to your mama before she curses me out. You know how she is when she's watching "Don't Be a Menace to South Central While Drinking Your Juice in The Hood."

"Yeah, I know. That's her favorite movie," I said, still thinking about what he'd just said to me.

"Fal, talk to the nigga. Me and Legend pulled up on the boy today, and that nigga is sick over you. He's solid as fuck though, I'll give him that," Fonzo said as he walked out of my room and closed the door.

I was now left alone with my thoughts. Fonzo had to be just talking shit, but damn, what all did his crazy ass really get into today? My thoughts were running wild and were completely all over the place. Kiyan was calling my phone back-to-back so much that I just put it on Do Not Disturb. I needed a moment of quiet right now. As I sat on my bed, it dawned on me that I couldn't remember the last time I had taken my birth control pills or had a period.

What the fuck Fallon?! "Please, not again!" I said so that only I could hear myself. I could not believe that I had fucked up this majorly! I grabbed my cell phone immediately because I needed to do some math. I had to find out when the last time was I'd had a period and who I slept with. This was about to seriously blow my mind. I wondered if pregnancy was the reason for my excessive eating, sleeping, and nausea as of late. I had written it all off as nerves and stress from everything that'd been going on lately. While going through text messages and the calendar on my phone, I figured that if I was indeed pregnant, I'd be at least two months along. The last time I took my birth control had been the day before my birthday. The issue was the paternity of the baby. It was between Kiyan and Torrance. Torrance. Shit, it'd completely just slipped my mind that Torrance was dead now, so if it was his baby, I would be horrified. I took one step in a positive direction today by enrolling in school. Now, here it was, I had yet another obstacle to get through. I really couldn't catch a break. I guess I'd be calling my doctor's office first thing in the morning. This had to be one sick joke being played on me. I was so tired that I didn't even change out of my clothes. I laid right down and went to sleep.

The next morning when I woke up, I was in no rush to go anywhere fast. I lingered in the bed for a few extra minutes. I noticed that I'd slept much longer than usual. It was eleven in the morning when I finally decided to roll out of the bed. I went in the bathroom to brush my teeth and wash my face, and that was when I heard voices coming from downstairs. Once I was finished, I followed the sounds and smells into the kitchen. This time, instead of my mother cooking, it was Fonzo. I had never even known him to cook, so this was a pleasant surprise. Another surprise, although not so pleasant, was that Legend was back again.

"Good morning, parents," I sang.

"Hey boo," Stormy said sweetly.

"Hey Pooh Butt, how did you sleep?" Papi asked.

"I slept alright, daddy," I told him.

"You look like you need another spa day, baby, are you sure you're okay?"

"Dang ma, do I look that bad?" I tried to laugh it off.

"You look fine to me," said the unwanted guest, standing at the island.

"Nobody asked you," I said and rolled my eyes.

"Fallon, be nice, and no, you do not look bad, I'm just saying, we can go whenever you'd like. Okay, baby?" Stormy jumped to the rescue. Legend just smirked with his annoying ass.

"Soooo," I changed the subject. "I have some news, guys. I enrolled in McColly's Real Estate School yesterday, and I start next month!" I said excitedly.

My parents were both really excited for me. Even Legend's punk ass showed some happiness for me. If I'm being honest, Legend really wasn't that bad. He was just extremely sexy, and I had to keep my distance and remember that he worked for my father. When the excitement from my news calmed down, Fonzo announced that it was time to eat. I was looking forward to seeing what Papi was able to do in the kitchen. He prepared an authentic Cuban dish, and it looked and smelled amazing. I asked him what he'd made, and he told me it was Picadillo Cua-Cua, also known as Cuban hash and eggs. My mother blessed the food, and as I was about to dig in, Fonzo cleared his throat and asked me if I was going to look into what he told me about last night. He caught me off guard, but I responded and told him yes, and he left it at that. Of course, Stormy wanted to know what we were talking about, but Papi saved me when he diverted her attention by asking her what wedding planning she was getting into today. *Whew!*

CHAPTER 30

I wasn't able to get in to see my doctor for two weeks. When I did finally see her, she confirmed what Fonzo speculated. I was indeed two months, well, nine weeks, pregnant. I had conceived sometime around my birthday and should be expecting to deliver sometime around early February. The craziest part about her findings was that upon my initial visit, during a routine ultrasound, she discovered that I was carrying twins. Fucking twins! How?!

Just when I thought that I was about to get my life together, karma said, "Haha bitch, go somewhere and sit down. Like, for nine months!"

That day when I walked out of the doctor's office, I felt like I'd been hit with déjà vu. The only difference was that this time, I didn't have any doubts about whether I was going to keep my babies or not. I still felt remorse about the last abortion; I wasn't putting myself through that again.

I was told that the police didn't have any suspects in Torrance's murder and that his family gave him a memorial service last week. There had been rumors that Kiyan had something to do with it. I didn't attend for obvious reasons. I never brought the conversation up to Papi either. I don't even feel bad about him being killed anymore.

I'd only hoped that my babies didn't turn out to be his. I wasn't going to worry about that right now, though.

I did need to have a sit down with Kiyan and tell him what was going on. He deserved to know one way or the other. He had been calling me every day but, I wasn't ready to talk. There was nothing to say — until today. So, I did what was necessary and called Kiyan. He answered the phone on the second ring.

"Hello?"

"Kiyan, are you busy? Because I need to talk to you," I said with an attitude.

Without hesitation, he said, "Pull up then, Fal, I'm at the crib."

Shit. Shit. Shit, I thought. I told him that I was on my way and hung up the phone.

I took my sweet ass time driving to Kiyan's house, partially because this was a conversation that I didn't think I was ready for. Also, because I hadn't seen or spoken to Kiyan since the blowup we had, which led me to being choked. It could very well just be my nerves, but whatever it was, I was in no rush to get to him.

Unfortunately for me, the ride was much shorter than I'd anticipated, even with me stopping for a Dunkin' Donuts' blueberry pomegranate refresher. I thought about driving right back off and attempting this another day, but I needed to put on my big girl panties. If not for me, I had to do it for Baby A and Baby B, who were growing inside of me.

Before I could even pick up my phone to let Kiyan know that I was outside, he called to let me know that the door was open. I looked up to see how he had even known I was there, and that's when I noticed the cameras around the building that hadn't been there before. He was also standing in the window watching me.

"Of course, he's watching me walk the walk of shame," I said to myself. "Here we go," I groaned.

When I made it inside the house, I noticed that it was a little more on the messy side, which wasn't like Kiyan at all. I walked a little further and there he was, sitting on the couch, with no shirt on, waiting for me. I'd be a damn fool not to notice how good Kiyan looked right now. He had often been told that he resembled the rapper, Dave East. It was times like now where I could see it.

"Hey," I said.

"What's up, Fal, you good?" he asked.

"Yeah, I'm good, I guess. I just had to holler at you about some things," I said.

"Aight, shoot," he said and lit the blunt that was on the table in front of him.

"Um, can you hold off on that until I leave, please?" I asked him.

"Uhh, yeah I can, I guess," he replied confused.

"Thanks," I told him. "I won't be long."

"First, are you ok? You never let your house get like this."

Kiyan chuckled and said, "Damn Fallon, you act like my shit is nasty or something. A nigga been going through some things, and I haven't gotten around to cleaning up."

"What are you going through, nigga?" I joked.

He laughed and replied, "Well, where should I start? I lost my girl, these niggas out here in the streets tried me, and now I don't know what my next move is, Fallon. Then, I got your damn daddy on my ass. I ain't scared of Fonzo, but I respect the O.G., and he made me realize that I could've handled you better."

"Well, damn," was my only reply.

"Wait. What happened with my daddy? What did he say? Or do?" I asked.

"Nothing, he pulled up on me with some country ass nigga in the car. He just hollered at me man to man about the shit between me and you. Told me, if I ever put my hands on you again, he wouldn't be in the mood to talk next time. Then, he told me to get in the car so that we could handle that bitch ass nigga Torrance once and for all."

"Your Pops even sent a word out to get that nigga Jay touched," he told me.

"Oh My God!" I gasped. So, the rumors are true, then. You and my father did that to Torrance?" I asked, even though I kind of figured as much.

"I ain't gon' lie, Fal. That was the most fun I had in a long time.

Your pops really be on some sinister ass shit, and that country ass nigga is a lot crazier than he looks. That nigga Torrance had shit twisted if he thought that he would get away with the hoe ass shit he pulled with you," Kiyan expressed.

It should have bothered me that he was smiling while telling me this story, or even the fact that he was telling this to me at all. It didn't, though. These niggas were down for me. This was MY team, and I felt a sense of pride. Even Legend's ass, who was new to the scene, was with the shits. Why did Kiyan's involvement in criminal activities make my panties wet? This was bad, Fallon, really bad.

CHAPTER 31

When Kiyan was done telling me about all that transpired with him, my father, and Torrance, he realized that I'd yet to tell him what I'd actually come to talk to him about. He asked, "Enough about what I had going on. What did you want to talk to me about?" It was now or never.

"Well, Kiyan," I started. "I never thought that this would be something we'd have to deal with, especially with our current situation, but I found out that I'm pregnant. Again."

Kiyan just blankly stared at me before he responded. "Ok, and?"

"And," I continued, "I didn't realize that I wasn't taking my pills the way that I was supposed to. There was so much going on at the time."

"Fallon, get to the fucking point, because if it's mine, you know how I'm coming. So, what's the problem?" Kiyan was becoming annoyed, so I got to the point.

"Ok, the issue is that I conceived around my birthday, and I was sleeping with you and Torrance. I can't be sure who the father is." I had finally gotten it all out.

Kiyan lit the blunt that was on the table and took several long pulls off of it. He was pissed. "Fallon," Kiyan said, literally blowing smoke. I proposed to you on your birthday, and you mean to tell me that you were fucking a nigga raw when you accepted my ring, Joe?"

Oh shit, here we go! I chose not to trigger him this time, so I remained calm when I spoke.

"Yes, Kiyan, and I'm sorry," I said genuinely.

Kiyan looked at me and I saw pain in his eyes once again.

"Hold up, did you say that you conceived around your birthday?"

"Yes."

"Yo, that was like two months ago?"

"Yes, it was. The doctor says I'm roughly nine weeks pregnant." Kiyan got eerily quiet and picked up his phone. He was inputting something and reading it in what looked to be Google.

After a few more moments of silence, Kiyan stood up and walked towards me. Now the last time he did that, I ended up being choked out, so for every step he took towards me, I took two steps back.

This crazy ass man had the nerve to ask me if he was making me nervous. *Duh, nigga! You won't get me like that again,* I thought.

"I'm not about to hurt you, Fallon. I'll never put my hands on you again. I want to show you something," he said.

"Ok, but Kiyan, do not try me. What is it that you want me to see?"

"How serious are you about figuring out the paternity of the baby?" he asked.

"Kiyan, that's not even a serious question. I'd love nothing more than to know."

I truly meant that too.

"Bet, then look at this," he said.

"NIPT?" I asked. "What is that?"

"It's a fairly new procedure called Non-Invasive Paternity Testing. NIPT. We can get it done as early as nine weeks, and it's supposed to be 99.9% accurate. It's a blood draw through your arm, and there's no risk of harming the baby. The results come back via email in seven days," he explained.

"That is a lot to take in, Kiyan," I said. "Are you sure that there won't be any risks?"

"From what I'm reading, it's supposed to be harmless to you and the baby."

"Ok, I guess. Call and set it up," I told him.

The truth was that I wanted to know myself, so if there was a way of us finding out without the twins or myself being harmed, I was down for it. While Kiyan took care of that, I helped myself to food I saw in the kitchen. One thing about this pregnancy thus far, was that I was always hungry. I ended up helping myself to the barbecue from I-57, a well known Barbecue joint in Chicago which was on the counter. I was stuffing my face when Kiyan came in the kitchen with the details of our appointment.

"Damn Joe, I didn't tell your hungry ass to come eat up all my food," he said.

"Nigga, who was going to stop me?" I asked.

"Aight, you got that," he laughed. He informed me that the appointment was for the next day at ten in the morning. I told him that I would just meet him up there, but he insisted on picking me up.

"Kiyan, we are not cool. I don't need you picking me up to take me anywhere," I sassed.

"Girl, shut up! If you are about to be my baby mama again, you better get used to this shit," he told me.

"I'm not getting used to shit! Nothing between us will change, nigga! I still don't like you."

"Yeah right; you cappin'!" He was laughing at me.

"I don't know why you think that," I said. "Why do you think this is a game?"

"Because you're still wearing my ring."

I was speechless. He was right, though. Every time I took the ring off, I would put it right back on. I'm not sure what it was, but I felt like me keeping it off was officially admitting that it was really over. It was now time for me to go. I'd said what I needed to say. Everything else was extra. Before I realized that, I'd been deep inside of my thoughts, and by the time that I snapped out of it Kiyan was in my face kissing me. It was a gentle and reassuring kiss. It felt so damn good too! I broke it and backed away from him quickly.

"Kiyan, I have to go," I spoke. I'll see you in the morning."

"I'll be at your door at nine-fifteen, baby mama." He was smiling.

I rolled my eyes as I headed to the door. I didn't leave, however, until I said just one last thing. "Hey, Kiyan?"

"Yes, Mrs. McDade?" Now he was just being obnoxious, but I continued.

"I just thought that you should know one more thing about this pregnancy." I had his full attention by then, so I told him, "The baby, is actually babies." I smiled.

"What are you talking about, Fal?" he stammered.

"I'm pregnant with twins," I said as I stuck my middle finger up and walked out of the door. The look on his face was priceless, and I laughed all the way to my car.

CHAPTER 32

When I got inside of my car, my stomach still felt empty, as if I didn't just get done eating. This time, I had an actual craving. I wanted some fried catfish fillets, baked macaroni and cheese, and candied yams. I knew just where to go to fulfill my appetite. I called Midwest Eats in East Chicago and ordered my meal to go. My plan was to go home, eat, and tell my mother and father about the new additions that would be making their imprint on our lives in the next seven months. One thing that my doctor had warned me about was preterm delivery, was that most multiples come before the expected delivery date. That was fine with me, just as long as they gave their mama enough time to fully prepare for their arrival.

I was in and out of the restaurant and on my way home in no time. When I pulled up to my mother's house, there was only one car in the driveway, but I didn't recognize it. My mother usually parked her car in the garage, so I was being nosey at this point. I walked into the living room to find my mother and another lady sitting on the couch with over a dozen bridal books spread out in front of them. Stormy looked so happy. I didn't want to interrupt, so I peeked in and waved to my mom before heading to my bedroom.

I chilled out in my room, eating and scrolling through my social media accounts, until I heard a soft knock at the door. "Come in," I yelled. It was the beautiful Stormy.

"Hey gorgeous," she sang.

"Hey yourself, beautiful," I reciprocated.

"What's new with you, boo?!" she said, attempting to be cool.

"Ma, you're so lame for that." We both laughed.

"Girl whatever," my mother said.

"Anyway, Ma, guess what?" I was so excited to spill this tea.

"What girl?"

"I'm sorry to burst your bubble, girlfriend, but you're going to be a grandma!" I was half joking, half serious.

"Girl, I know your ass is not pregnant!" she spoke.

The laughing stopped and I replied, "Yes ma, I am."

"Well, how far along are you, Fallon?"

"The doctor said around nine weeks," I answered.

"Oh, my goodness, Fallon! Well, you are grown now, so there isn't much I can say other than I love you, and you know that you have my full support."

Whew!

"So, you aren't mad?" I asked.

"I'm not mad, Fallon. You're a big girl and you were taught and raised well, so I know that you'll be fine. I just wish you would have waited just a little while longer. There is so much life that you haven't experienced yet, you know? A baby isn't going to hold you back from anything, though. If you prioritize things the right way, you can still achieve everything you set your mind too. You also have a big support system. Your ass better fit into your dress next May for my wedding, though. I'll just have to plan something extra special to include my new grandbaby!" she gushed.

"Um ma, there's just this one thing, though," I said, biting my nail.

"What?"

"Grandbabies. I'm having twins," I said.

"Well shit, baby! I need a damn glass of wine now," she said.

"I'll also have you know that ain't no damn body calling me grand-nothing! I'm still young and sexy, so they will call me Glam-Ma or Glammy. I'll let you know which one I decide to go with."

Stormy Swilley, soon-to-be Jax, was a force to be reckoned with, chile, I laughed to myself.

"Ma, where's my dad?" I asked, ready to tell him that he was right all along.

"They released two of your brothers today, so he went and picked them up. He'll be home later," she replied on her way out.

Damn, they are really letting them all back onto the streets. The Jax family is about to be back and stronger than ever now.

CHAPTER 33

I barely slept a wink last night. I was super nervous about the paternity test and its results. Just the thought of knowing that Kiyan could very well not be the father had my stomach in knots. I decided to listen to some music while I got ready for the appointment. I felt like listening to H.E. R today. Her vibe was just what I needed to settle my nerves a bit. The first song that played was *Changes*. Who would've guessed that the lyrics in that song would relate to my life the way they did? Along with my baby daddy drama, I was battling the mixed feelings and emotions that I had for Kiyan. I felt as though I really fucked things up between us by being selfish. I also kept thinking about school. I was set to start school in one week, and as much as I still wanted to be able to complete the program, with two new babies coming, would I have the time? I had to tackle one issue at a time, however, so I had to focus on the issue at hand first. I was done getting dressed and went down to the kitchen because I knew there would be food there. My mother, father, and my two oldest brothers, King and Chino, were at the table eating. Legend ended up coming out of the bathroom also. They were down here licking fingers and plates, meanwhile, I was upstairs with hunger pangs.

"Well, good morning, everyone," I said a little salty. I heard a bunch of mumbles, and then there were my parents, the only two I was able to understand clearly.

"Hey baby," they spoke.

"I sholl hope there's more to eat in the house, with the way that y'all are tearing those plates up," I giggled.

"Man, shut up and sit your ass down by me, big head! Tell me what nigga out here I gotta fuck up behind you," King said.

Before I could respond, Fonzo jumped in and said, "Not a damn soul, son. You know I took care of that bullshit as soon as it hit my nose!"

"Aww yeah, Papi, true!" Chino chimed in.

I just looked at my mother and we both smiled and rolled our eyes. We were definitely outnumbered. The laughs and shit talking continued. I ate a couple bites of food before my phone buzzed, alerting me that Kiyan was outside.

"Where are you going?" Chino asked.

"To see a man about a dog," I said and walked out.

"Yeah, ok!" I heard them all say.

I peeked back in to say, "Hey boys, we need to have dinner this week. I have something that I want to share with all of you."

Fonzo assured me that he would set it up, and I left out.

When I got inside of Kiyan's car, I could smell that he'd tried to mask the smell of weed. The effort was cute, although he didn't do a very good job.

"What's up?" I said while putting my seatbelt on.

"I can't call it. How are you feeling, though?" he asked.

"I'm ok. Just ready to get this over with," I told him.

"Yeah, I feel that."

After that small exchange, Kiyan turned the music up, and we rode in silence. I was in my thoughts, and I could tell that Kiyan was in his as well. It took us a few hours to get to our destination. When Kiyan stopped the car, neither of us moved to get out. We both sat still, staring at the brick building. We both knew that after this test, our lives would forever be changed —whether for the good or bad. All of the suspense was killing me, so I made the first move and got out with Kiyan following suit. We walked side by side into the lab and was greeted by a staff member. Once we filled out the necessary paperwork, it was finally time for the blood draw. The doctor explained the process further and answered any questions we may have had. I know that I had a couple. Dr. Lynn was really friendly and thorough.

It literally took no more than a few minutes to do. When Dr. Lynn told us that we were free to go, I felt a little relief. Now the waiting game started. Kiyan asked Dr. Lynn as we walked out if there was a way to expedite the test results. She surprised us both by ensuring us that we could get an answer back within the next three days. There was, of course, an extra fee added on for that, but Kiyan didn't care. He needed to know what was going on as soon as possible. I did too. We made it back to the car and there was, once again, more silence. It was cool though, because what do you really say to a person after having to do something like that? So, Kiyan turned the music back on, started the car back up, and we drove back towards my house. Before we made it all the way, Kiyan turned the music down and asked if I was hungry. My answer was yes, of course. We went to Beggars Pizza. After the waitress came with our food and drink order, Kiyan decided to really break the ice.

"Outside of the baby situation, what else have you been up to? You've definitely been curving me," he asked.

"I wasn't curving you, Kiyan. I just needed some time to get myself together, and that's exactly what I did. I finally figured out what I wanted to do with my life, and I enrolled in McColly Real Estate School," I told him truthfully.

Kiyan smiled that sexy smile of his and said, "That's what I'm talking about! Boss up then, shorty!"

I laughed, but it felt good to be able to tell him and hear his reaction.

CHAPTER 34

"When do you start school?" he asked.

"Actually, in one week," I told him. "I'm nervous as all hell too."

"Nervous for what? You got this, girl! You're one of the smartest people I know. I was actually thinking about buying a few buildings. Maybe you can help me with that process once you complete your program."

"I might be able to help, but I still don't fuck with you like that," I joked. We both laughed and the rest of our time at the restaurant went smoothly. We ate, laughed, and talked shit to each other the way that we did in the beginning of our relationship. It felt really good to be able to be happy and carefree around Kiyan. The last few months had been so rough, we barely enjoyed one another's presence. I didn't even want to ruin the vibe with my thoughts, so I tuned back into Kiyan for the remainder of our impromptu lunch date.

After about an hour and a half at Beggars, Kiyan finally took me back home. It was a bittersweet moment. I didn't really want the day to end, but until we got the results back, it was probably best that we kept our distance from one another. We both sat in front of the house for a second, trying to think of something to say. I decided to speak first by thanking Kiyan for lunch.

He just had to pull me into my feelings by saying, "Anything, anytime for you, Fallon."

I blushed and turned to get out of the car, and that was when he asked me for a hug. "I don't think that's a good idea, Kiyan," I said.

"Why not, Fallon? It's just a hug," he tried to reason.

"Because Kiyan, I don't know if it's the hormones or not, but when you touch me, I feel things. I don't want to do that, at least not right now. We need to figure out what's happening with these babies first," I explained honestly.

"I feel you, Fal, but you're the only one who has something to figure out. I'm here. Whether those babies have my blood running through their veins or not, they're my shorties. I want to know for sure or not, just for my own sanity, but we got two babies coming into this world regardless. Why don't you comprehend that I still love you? You will still carry my last name one day, Fallon."

I couldn't believe what I was hearing right now. Why was Kiyan saying all of these things? He had to just be fucking with me.

"Kiyan, stop playing with me. You don't have to say shit like that if you don't mean it. That's a big commitment to make, and I wouldn't even put that kind of pressure on you if these aren't your babies."

I needed Kiyan to understand that he didn't have to do me any favors. "Listen Kiyan, go home and think about what you just said. If you still feel the same way when the results come back, then I'll be willing to have a real discussion with you about it. Just remember that we had other issues before this pregnancy. All of it would need to be addressed before we entertained the thought of moving forward. Okay?"

Kiyan looked me dead in my eyes and said, "Aight, Fal, I hear you, Joe. Just do me one solid?"

"What's that, Kiyan?" I asked.

"Just don't take that ring off."

"Ok Kiyan, now bye." I said, exiting the car and damn near running into the house. I had to close the door quickly before I ran back to his car and give in to him.

I didn't know what had gotten into Kiyan, but he was making me nervous. That was some heavy shit that he laid on me. What was even worse was that I kind of believed every word he said. I didn't realize just how much Kiyan was willing to do for me until now. I didn't know what to do or think about any of it. Even if I was willing to work things out with him, there was still the issue of Terica's rat ass and the lingering "what ifs" surrounding the paternity of the babies. I just wouldn't feel comfortable allowing Kiyan to take on a father role to kids that weren't his. This was really a moment where I wished I could have a drink. I needed a shot badly right now.

Once I got my bearings together, I walked into the living room, and to my surprise, there wasn't a house full of people. I think this was the first time that I had been in the house alone in a while. It was way too quiet in here, so I decided to take advantage of it. I sat back on the couch, turned the TV on, and got comfortable. I must've gotten too comfortable because I was awakened by a pillow being thrown at my head. Damn. That was a good ass nap too, but now I was irritated because it was disturbed by none other than Legend.

"Dawg, what the fuck is wrong with you? Why would you wake me up?!" I yelled.

"Because it's too early to be on some sleepy shit. Get yo' ass up, shawty," he said, laughing at himself.

"Legend, why the fuck are you even here? My father isn't here, so what do you want?!" I asked him, highly annoyed.

"Aww shawty, you must not have gotten the memo. I'll be your new houseguest for a while."

"Why?" I asked. "Don't you have somewhere else you could be?"

"Nope. Your pops asked me to look after you and your OG when he's not able to, so here I am."

"I don't like you," I told him.

"Aww girl, you gon' end up loving a nigga one day. You need to stop playing and let me break your back in. Yo ass always walking around tense and shit. You need some of this country wood," he said and walked out.

"You got me fucked up! You'll never get none of this, nigga!" I yelled behind him. It didn't matter because he was already gone.

"Aargh!" I screamed into the pillow that was thrown at me.

Legend and all of his fineness could not be under the same roof as me. I'd end up putting this whole entire pregnant pussy on his face, and I just didn't need those problems right now. I was in recovery mode. Once I calmed down, I went into the kitchen and grabbed some of the fresh, cut up fruit we had and went to my room. Hopefully, there I wouldn't be bothered by the houseguest from hell.

I decided to call Tia just to see what she was up to. It was so crazy to me that we'd ended up being pregnant together. I was going to be sad when she moved. I understood that she was doing what was best for her and the family she was creating, but I was about to lose my best friend. After the third ring, I hung up the phone. I wondered what she was doing and why she didn't pick up the phone.

I was officially bored, so I did the next best thing I could think of — shopping. I didn't know the gender of my babies yet, so there wasn't much I could do with that outside of neutral colors. I figured since I would be pregnant for most of the fall and winter months, I'd opt for cute sweaters, leggings, and sweater dresses instead of buying maternity clothing. When I was satisfied with my purchases, I started googling what to expect during pregnancy. Some of those videos and stories creeped me out, so I stopped. As soon as I put my phone down, it rang. It was Tia, calling me back. I was excited to hear from her, so when I answered, I started our normal routine.

"What's up, bitchhhhhh!" I sang.

CHAPTER 35

"Hey Fallon, girl," she said, but her voice was somber.

"Uht Uh, what's wrong, T?" I asked.

"Girl, last night Me and Deno had to come to the hospital because I was having some really bad pains in my pelvic area. By the time we made it here, I'd started spotting."

"Oh no, Tia!" I said to her.

"Yeah, the doctors ran their tests, and I had an ultrasound, which revealed that the baby's little heartbeat wasn't there anymore," Tia cried.

"I'm so sorry, best friend. Is there anything I can do for you?" I asked.

"No, friend. I'll be okay. I was really excited about this baby!"

"I know, friend. I know," I consoled.

"Me and Deno decided to still go ahead with our move. We'll just try again," she said.

"Okay, well if you need me, I'm here. Do you want me to come up to the hospital?" I asked.

"No, friend. I just need some time to take it all in. I'll call you when I get discharged."

"Ok girl, I love you!"

"I love you too, Fal," she said.

My heart literally broke for my friend. She was so excited about the baby and being a mom. I definitely couldn't tell her that I was pregnant. Then, to add insult to injury, I wasn't just having one baby, I was having two? I decided to keep that news to myself when dealing with her until she was in a better state of mind. I was now back to being bored with no one to talk to. It was getting late, so I decided to take a warm bubble bath, using my Dr. Teal's sleep soak and take my butt to bed. It would be a long next few days until the test results came back. I had to keep myself busy until then to keep from reaching out to Kiyan.

Over the course of the three day wait, I did any and everything to stay busy. I shopped, helped my mother with wedding plans, read books, and caught up on TV shows. I didn't realize how much time I had on my hands without running the streets. I should've enrolled into my classes a long time ago just to have something to do. Surprisingly, Baby A and Baby B were being good to their mama. I had only gotten sick that one time before I had even known that I was pregnant. Based on the videos that I'd seen and stories that I'd read, I was doing pretty well.

I had been cleaning and rearranging my bedroom when I got a text message from Kiyan telling me that Dr. Lynn had called with the results. She wanted to tell us both simultaneously, so he asked if I could come over, so we could call Dr. Lynn back together. I threw my shoes on so fast, I hadn't realized I'd put on two different Ugg Slides until Stormy asked me what was wrong with me on my way to the front door. When I looked down and noticed what she was referring to, I ran back up the stairs to find two slides that matched. *Get it together, Fallon,* I pep talked myself on my way back down the stairs.

This time, Stormy stood at the door, waiting for me. "Fallon, are you okay?" she asked.

"Yes ma, I was just moving too fast. I guess its pregnancy brain," I said.

"Umm hmm, well slow your ass down, baby girl," she said and walked off.

The drive to Kiyan's house was torturous. I didn't even pay attention to the fact that I was speeding until I happened to glance at my speedometer. I knew I was tripping, because the police in Lake County do not play. I definitely didn't want those problems today, so I slowed my ass all the way down. My mind was racing, however. What would I really do if these babies did not truly, fully belong to Kiyan? Then, how would I explain it to them when they got older? What would I say? "Oh yeah, babies, your mama was out here hoeing and your grandpa, his irritating, country ass friend, and the man who should've been your daddy killed him."

Whyyyyyy did I put myself in these types of predicaments? It had to be mental illness, I thought to myself. It was as if my life was right off of a scene from a Murda Pain hood movie.

In the midst of my silly ass thoughts, I pulled up to Kiyan's house. I don't even remember putting my car in park all the way before I hopped out of it. I hit Kiyan's threshold with the speed of Usain Bolt! All I knew was that I needed Dr. Lynn on the line expeditiously! Kiyan was standing in the living room, laughing at me. I could only assume that he must've been watching me the whole time, and I didn't even care.

"Call her!" I said out of breath.

"Ok, lil' thirsty, I am. Calm down," he said, still laughing. I didn't see anything funny.

Kiyan called the lab and we waited for Dr. Lynn to come on the line. He tried to get me to relax by bringing me a bottle of water and massaging my shoulders. He didn't get it, though; I wouldn't relax until I knew what was going on. I really did hate how calm and nonchalant Kiyan was being. How was he not as antsy and nervous as me? Maybe he had gotten high. Shit, maybe I should hit that shit one time to rest my nerves. That actually sounded like a good idea in my head, so I leaned over to reach for the blunt that was on the table, but Kiyan smacked it out of my hand. I laughed, but it really pissed me off because he smacked that shit like when you pick something up from off of the ground and your mama sees you then smacks it because you don't know where it came from or where it's been.

"Kiyan, what the fuck?" I whispered.

"Fallon, you got me fucked up," was all he said before Dr. Lynn came on the line.

CHAPTER 36

"Hi guys! I'm sorry to have kept you waiting. The lab has been getting hit with new clients ever since the word has gotten out about us. Ok, let's see what we have here for you guys," she said. "Are you scared, nervous, or excited?" she asked.

Since I was becoming annoyed by the small talk, Kiyan spoke up and answered her. "Yeah Doc, we're good, we just want to get to it, ya feel me?"

"Oh, I definitely understand, I'm just reviewing things now," she said. "Okay, so what we have here is a positive match here for you, Mr. McDade."

That was all I needed before I broke down in tears. I was so happy for this news. I looked up and saw Kiyan smiling his big sexy smile, and that was all of the confirmation I needed. I almost tuned Dr. Lynn out completely — that is, until I heard her ask if we wanted to know the gender of the babies.

"Wait! Did you say that you also knew the genders?" I asked. Now I was willing to speak to her ass.

"Yes, Ms. Jax." Would you two like to know?" she asked us.

We both looked at each other and answered "Yes!" In unison.

"Ok, well, it looks as if you two will be welcoming twin girls into your family. Congratulations you guys, you really are a sweet couple!" she said.

"Thank you, Dr. Lynn!" we sang and Kiyan disconnected the call.

I was the first to speak and I looked at Kiyan in shock, "Oh, my God! We are having twin girls! Can you believe that?"

"Man, hell no, I thought I'd at least finally get one boy out of the deal," he told me.

I laughed and said, "Not today, nigga!"

Kiyan had the audacity to look at me and say, "Don't trip. I know that you got me on the next round, ain't that right?" I had to look at the remainder of the blunt on the table because Kiyan was obviously high if he thought that I would be getting pregnant again!

"Kiyan, I'm not having any more damn kids. You're lucky to get these two. We got a two for one deal right here."

He must've thought I was joking or something because his only response was, "We'll see."

"There is no 'we'll see,' I'm telling you, this is it!"

Kiyan walked up to me, grabbed me by the waist, and pulled me in for a kiss. Surprisingly, this time, I let it happen. I didn't even pull away this time. I was feeling so euphoric after the news we received from Dr. Lynn. When Kiyan attempted to pull my jeggings down, I put a halt to that.

"No, we are not doing that right now," I said.

"Come on, bae, we just got all of the confirmation we needed. Now let me get some of that," he begged.

"Kiyan, no!" There are still things that we need to talk about," I said, pushing him away.

"Fallon, we literally have forever to talk. Come here, bae."

Kiyan was horny, that much I could see. The dick print poking through his basketball shorts almost made my mouth water. I held my ground, though. He was not sticking his penis inside of me until we had everything between us figured out. Not fully communicating was a part of the problems we had that brought us to this point anyway.

"Urggghhh! Ok, Fal, what's up? What is it that you want to talk about?" Kiyan said, clearly frustrated.

"Thank you. For starters, we need to come up with some sort of plan, because once I have these babies, I'll need to finish school," I told him.

"Ok bet, I'll need to keep the babies while you're at school. That's simple, what else?

"Kiyan, it is not that simple, you can't take my kids out on the block with you," I told him.

"Fallon, I know that. I am not new to this shit, I got them," he replied.

"See, that's another issue I have. Kiyan, I get that I'll have to get over some of the things that happened between us, but the Terica situation still burns me up on the inside."

"Fallon, I know that I hurt you with that, but there isn't a Terica situation at this point. I take care of Kiyari and that's it. Terica knows what's up. She knows that you're going to be my wife. I fucked up, I know, but I never did that shit again."

"I hear you, Kiyan, I really do, but my emotions are all over the place right now. Like, how do I know that you didn't cater to Terica during her pregnancy the way you trying to do with me? How do I know that you won't do it again? Because the next time, I'll have to kill you. See, I'm threatening you for shit that hasn't even happened. I'm not stable," I laughed.

"Fallon, bae, listen. Now as much as I love Kiyari, her being here wasn't something that was supposed to happen, at least not with Terica. But, she's here. Terica isn't the one that I'm supposed to be with, cater to, none of that. You are. I love you and all of your fucked up ways, Fallon. Can't nobody change that, Joe. You do have to know and accept that Kiyari is a part of our family too, though," Kiyan stressed.

"Ok. So, what do we do now? We're actually about to be parents," I asked.

"I should be asking you that question, bae. You're the one who holds all of the cards, Joe."

"I'm willing to try if you are. We have to communicate, though — whether the other person wants to hear it or not. I'm going to put my all into this, Kiyan. Please don't make me regret it," I told him.

"Fallon, I been right here, just waiting for this moment. Real niggas need love too," he joked. "But seriously, I got you, us, and them forever. We're locked in for life, baby. Now all you have to do, is tell me that you're trying to be Mrs. McDade again. For real this time."

I was in tears. Kiyan had melted my heart.

"Yes baby, I am willing to be Mrs. McDade again, for real this time."

"That's what the fuck I'm talking about, bae! But um, no disrespect to your pops and your O.G., but you gotta bring your ass home now!" Kiyan said with a straight face.

"What are you talking about, Kiyan?" I asked genuinely confused. He explained, "You aren't living in your parents' house pregnant with my babies. Let's go get your shit, 'cause you're coming home!"

"Kiyan, I hear you, but this place is not big enough for the both of us, the twins, and Kiyari," I explained.

"Fallon, I don't care. I got your back, and it's my job to make sure that y'all are good," he said.

"I understand," I told him. If that's the case, I'll do that, but you need to buy us a bigger house before the twins get here. Just remember that I'm extra as hell, so you better have your coins together. You're a girl dad now, so everything will be big, pink, and expensive. Me and your three daughters are going to whoop your ass," I laughed.

"Girl, I ain't no broke nigga! Challenge accepted!" he said. "Shit, me and Papi made a couple of moves to secure us for a lifetime. We good over here, baby. You just do your job, beautiful," he smirked.

"What job is that, fool?"

"Well, I'm not the one going to McColly, you are. So, while you're over there talking about this big ass house you want then find it, Miss Realtor."

"Cool with me. Say less," I said.

"Aight now bae, since we got all of that out of the way, can I get some pussy now, please?

"Come on, Daddy. Let me rock that mic before I get too big to do so," I told him.

EPILOGUE

10 MONTHS LATER

Today is the day that my mother became Mrs. Stormy Jax. The ceremony was absolutely beautiful! Both of my parents were breathtaking, and everyone in attendance was full of emotion. My father had all of his closest associates and all five of his sons at his side. Well, six, since Kiyan and I got married on Valentine's Day, which was three months ago. My mother had everyone by her side as well. Even a very pregnant Tia came into town from Atlanta to be a part of my mother and father's special day. Kiyari was the cutest flower girl ever. I still talked shit to Stormy about getting married one week before my damn birthday, and her response was always," Fallon, ain't nobody thinking about your ass. You are grown with your own kids now! I'll get married in whatever month I want to!"

I shook my head at the thought that my mama will forever be a shit talker. She and my father decided to take an extended honeymoon since it took them so long to finally get their shit together. They were headed to the Maldives of Greece in the morning and wouldn't be returning for eight weeks. I'm sure they'd be face-timing me every single day to see the girls.

Kiyan and I decided not to wait once the twins were born to get married. They came a few weeks earlier than my original February fifth due date. They were healthy, so that they only stayed in the hospital for a few extra days after their birth. They were so cute and chunky. We decided to name them Storie Xiomara and Dream Mozelle after the two strong women who raised my parents. Storie ended up with both of my mother's colored eyes, while my Dreamy had one gray eye and one brown eye. That was really the only thing that would help you distinguish the difference between the two babies. They were both little dolls and the spitting images of Kiyan. Storie and Dream were beyond spoiled rotten already. If it wasn't one of my parents, my granny, or one of my brothers, then it was Kiyan or myself all in their faces, holding them.

For some strange reason, the sex and intimacy between Kiyan and me were off the charts. We couldn't keep our hands off of one another nor could we stand to be away from each other for too long. I learned my lesson with birth control pills, so I had a Mirena IUD inserted after the twins were born. Kiyan had me fucked up if he thought that I was going to become the Little Old Woman Who Lived in the Shoe. No sir.

I did get my dream home. We found it in Dyer, Indiana. Its exterior is stone and was made like a castle. We fell in love with it the very first time we saw it! I, of course, did the interior decorating and designed it perfectly for our little family.

Tia was finally able to get her happily ever after and was due in the next couple of weeks. She definitely cursed me out for holding out on telling her about my pregnancy. When I explained my reasoning to her, she understood, but assured me that she wasn't so selfish that she wouldn't have been happy for me.

I ended up taking the accelerated course for school and passing with high scores. I still had to work for a big company for one year before I could venture out on my own and start up my own real estate agency, but that was fine with me. Kiyan and my father had been doing good business together and money was flowing. I had even assisted in a few investments deals with Kiyan, so we now owned multiple properties throughout the Midwest and were looking to expand.

Terica decided that she really didn't want to be a full-time parent and she'd rather dance full time in the Miami strip clubs, so she signed over all of her legal rights to us. We now had Kiyari full time. I think she was happier with us anyway.

Legend and I had even ended our unspoken beef between each other. I guess once he figured out that I wasn't going to give up any pussy, we became cool. He's actually really funny.

My granny eventually came around to Fonzo. I guess she figured that he really wasn't going anywhere, so for my mother's sake, she let bygones be bygones. My Girl even found herself a "little friend" that she met on the boat. His name was Mr. Charles. He was a pretty smooth old man; I could tell that he was a looker back in his day. Everything was going beautifully. I was no longer "Faulty Fallon" but Fallon Jax-McDade, the woman. Hell, you could even call me Fallon 2.0 if you'd like, just to add a little spice to it.

I was learning and growing daily. I didn't let anything that could've brought me down succeed, and for that, I was damn proud.

Made in the USA
Monee, IL
13 July 2021